Lifting
the
Wheel
of
Karma

Lifting the Wheel of Karma

A Profound Spiritual Journey
of Extraordinary Healing and Redemption

A NOVEL

PAUL H. MAGID

Point Dume Press

Library of Congress Cataloging-in-Publication Data

Magid, Paul H.
Lifting the wheel of karma : a profound spiritual journal of extraordinary
healing and redemption : a novel / Paul H. Magid. -- Manalapan, NJ :
Point Dume Press, c2012.
p. ; cm.
ISBN: 978-0-9840160-6-8 (print) ; 978-0-9840160-9-9 (ebk)
1. Spiritual life--Fiction. 2. Karma--Fiction. 3. Philosophy, Asian- -Fiction. 4.
Spiritual healing--Fiction. 5. Forgiveness--Fiction.
6. India--Fiction. 7. Montana--Fiction. I. Title.

PS3613.A3452 L54 2012   2011916383
813.6--dc23   1109

www.PaulHMagid.com

Cover Design by Paul H. Magid

Published in the United States of America
by Point Dume Press

A deeply affectionate thank you
to
Sharon, for being the Love Of My Life
And for making Happiness possible
&
My dearest friends,
For never letting me forget
That even if Laughter can't cure what ails you
It can sure make it easier to endure

Acknowledgments

It is only because of the supportive and nurturing teachers of The Peddie School, in Hightstown, NJ, who showed an uncertain young man the irrepressible joy of creating pithy provocative prose, that this novel even exists.

Secondly, everything I know about Montana is thanks to Toby and Jody Dahl, who opened their home to me on their horse ranch, Runamuk, in Roundup, Montana. It would be fair to say that without Toby taking the time to teach me about life in Montana, there wouldn't even be a Chapter 1 of which to speak.

Prologue

A young man is walking down a path
Heading in earnest toward the Light
His back is thick
His arms strong
He comes upon an elderly man
Nearly feeble and limping
He stops
And scoops the man in his arms
"Why," asks the old man
"are you stopping to carry me?
It will take you longer to reach the Light."
"Why," replies the young man
"have I been given this body so strong?
If I return empty handed,
I will only be sent back for you."
The old man nods his weary head
Before resting it on the young man's chest
"That is why you return Home so young,
and I, an old man."

Chapter 1

The harrowing landscape was a disorienting mix of darkness and hypnotic light that appeared to ignore the rules governing its path, causing the eye to question what it saw. Joseph, aged seventeen, ran through lush vegetation in the entangled forest as he wielded a sword in his left hand. The sword was of a thin steel with a curve that extended from the handle to the tip. Carved into the sides of the steel were ornate designs of unknown origin. The handle was made of ivory and was capped with a slightly oversized gold tip to make sure the pinky finger was held in place when in use— which it surely was to be now.

Joseph was barefoot and dressed in an animal's hide about his hips as he ran. He had an athlete's muscular build. His handsome face was flushed with blood coursing through his veins. Sweat poured from his brow, stinging his eyes. He wiped the sweat away with his free right hand as he jumped over a tree recently felled to block his path. His breathing was loud and deep and echoed through the cold air searing his lungs.

He looked back for his pursuers—three large, muscled warriors that were ten yards behind him and gaining. They ran in perfect single file formation. Dressed as he was, they had no body hair, no head hair, not even eyebrows. Standing over seven feet tall, they were clones of each other and dwarfed the otherwise sturdy, five-foot, ten-inch Joseph. Though their hands were empty of weapon, this did not deter their intent or pursuit.

Joseph struggled to run faster and managed to increase the distance between himself and the warriors chasing him. Moments later they simply ceased running and disappeared where they stood. The misty fog grew thick and the air colder, making his labored breaths visible with each exhalation.

As he came to a clearing, his chest heaved and he strained to breath. He surveyed the open terrain, trying to decide which way to go, but his decision was quickly moot as all three warriors, whom he had just so exhaustively outrun, suddenly materialized a dangerous eight feet in front of him. They now each held a sword of their own, much larger than the one Joseph possessed. The razor sharp blades of their swords, easily capable of cutting through bone, glistened in the tormenting light.

Knowing he was too exhausted to resume his fruitless flight, the three warriors slowly and deliberately maneuvered to form a tight circle around Joseph. A lone, involuntary tear streamed down his left cheek from the corner of his eye. Not because he knew that there was no escape, but because in all the years he had been fleeing them, the three warriors had never stepped up their attacks with such frequency or ferocity as they had so recently. They seemed to be on an ever-shrinking timetable of mission and Joseph was crumbling under the ascent of their assault.

His enemies attacked in unison with smothering speed. The first warrior on his left attacked with a two-handed overhead blow as his sword sliced swiftly through the air. The second warrior stepped back to give the third warrior room to move. Joseph's response to the overhead attack from the first warrior was a successful defense in a loud clash of metal, but this left his unprotected back turned toward the third warrior.

This deadly enemy could now most certainly have cut Joseph in two through the waist and put an end to this torment. Instead, he flipped his sword from his right hand to his left hand, curled his powerful right hand into a tight fist and drove it with penetrating fury into the small of Joseph's back along his spine.

Shock waves of pain, so piercing they prevented sound from escaping his throat, reverberated throughout Joseph's body as his powerful legs collapsed and his knees buckled to the earth below. Tears streamed down his face as his torso recoiled from the brutal assault. Time ceased to exist for Joseph as his body attempted to process and recover from the violence inflicted upon it.

Seconds passed.

The three warriors stood over Joseph without attacking or even moving.

More seconds passed.

Still the warriors did not move.

With Joseph still on his knees and his jaw jutted skyward, he vomited up blood.

As the blood spewed from his mouth, he bolted upright in bed and awoke from the nightmare.

He coughed several times to clear his throat and his mind from the nightmare. He labored to breath and calm himself down. After several moments his chest stopped heaving and his breathing returned to normal. Slowly, with a familiar defeated exhaustion, he surveyed his blood stained pajamas. He sighed, lowered his head, and quietly climbed out of bed.

Minutes later he stood in the shower as the water cascaded down over him and washed the blood from his body. With his left forearm pressed against the shower wall he lowered his head and broke down crying. He tried to stop, but the more he did the more his chest seized and the more violently he cried.

Downstairs, Joseph's mother stood at the kitchen sink cleaning dishes as she looked out the window to enjoy the beautiful expanse of the Montana country-side. Mrs. Connell would not live anywhere else given the chance. This southeastern corner of Montana was filled with foothill mountains of sandstone rim rock crowned with millions of tall ponderosa pine trees. Ponderosa pine was a slow growing, patient tree with long green needles. It was a determined species.

It could grow right out the top of a sandstone rock formation from just the smallest fissure, and as it grew, it would separate the rock by forcing the tiny hole in the rock to grow larger and accommodate the tree's growth.

Sandstone, geologically speaking, was an easily eroded rock formation that lent itself to rising ridges that were poetically followed by descending slopes, only to have another adjoining ridge rise up again, so that these majestic foothill mountains, rising and falling between one hundred and three hundred feet high, gave way to fertile native grass meadows.

These meadows would slope and fall lower and lower until finally the lowest slope would start back up the other side, and a hundred yards away the hill-side would climb to the next series of rock slopes to be covered by another forest of ponderosa pine trees. The darker green of the pine tree needles contrasted with the lighter shaded grasses below.

Directly outside Mrs. Connell's kitchen window was a meadow of improved pasture—a mix of Blue Grass, Crested Wheat, Alfalfa, and two-foot high Timothy Grass. The Connell ranch was over twenty thousand acres in all, but had just one hundred and fifty acres of improved pasture—grasses introduced via agriculture for its high nutritional content for the thirty horses in total that populated this horse ranch. The improved pasture grasses gave more pounds per acre of feed for the cattle and horses than the native grasses of Green Needle, Blue Bunch Wheatgrass, and June Grass.

The gentle spring breeze blew white blossoms from the three apple trees directly outside the window of Mrs. Bonnie Connell's house. This particular variety of apple tree didn't produce the big juicy apples full of sweetness when a person bit into them, but they were perfect for baking apple pie when enough sugar was added to them, and that suited Mrs. Connell just fine.

The Connell household, of course, had all the requisite conveniences of modern times but did not suffer the afflictions of modernity, and the patriarch of this tight knit family, Mr. John Connell, would not have it any other way. This region of Montana didn't even get electricity until the mid-1950s, and that sense of self-sufficiency was fostered by Mr. Connell into his two boys, Billy, who was aged nineteen, and his younger son, Joseph.

Mr. Connell stood six feet tall but seemed taller to all who knew him. He was a man who knew that when his time came, God-willing many years from now, his coffin was carried—a man as well liked and respected as he was would have no shortage of willing pallbearers to help him along on his journey.

He made sure his sons could do the basic things in life right and the rest would flow naturally. The work pickup truck for the ranch had an extended carrying bed with raised wooden side walls to be able to haul more dirt where needed to assorted locations, which was often. It was also more than thirty years old —ancient even by the hardiest of truck standards. Mr. Connell could afford a new truck. He could afford a fleet of new trucks thanks to owning and operating the largest bottling plant west of the Mississippi. But to his way of thinking a new truck didn't move dirt any better than an old creaky one and all the fancy new electronics made no difference to him.

His daily use pickup truck was more than ten years old, and could have benefited from expensive tires with thick treads, but to Mr. Connell that would just have let his judgment of the terrain beneath him get sloppy and dull while navigating his foothill mountains, and he would have none of that. The same went for his boys.

When it came to other people, Mr. Connell believed others always deserved a helping hand, just not a handout. He was no taskmaster; in fact, he possessed an understated dry wit. Years ago when an impatient ten year-old Joseph was in a hurry to get out from the front seat of his father's pickup truck, he pulled so hard on the door handle that it snapped off right in his impatient little hand. As a stunned Joseph looked over to his father, Mr. Connell calmly leaned over, raised the door latch for his son and said, "Here, let me unlock that for you."

Life in Montana was picturesque but not easy. The country's fourth largest state had a population of just a million people in a country of over three hundred million. The climate could alternate between extremes of temperature and beauty—once having changed eighty-seven degrees in one twenty-four hour period. While summer heat was typically sweltering, Mr. Connell could remember the time it snowed on the Fourth of July.

Owing to its isolation, life was simple but not lacking. Residents seemed to revel in having endless space to spread their wings as they saw fit without knocking into the wings of others, yet help from a neighbor was always guaranteed whenever needed.

Verbal communication between Montanans could be either respectfully restrained or purposefully penetrating. While more often the former than the latter, it was never composed of idle chatter. This minimalist sense of utility that permeated and animated all facets of life in Montana came naturally from living so close to the rhythms of life—where nothing was used up wastefully.

Guns were a way of life here and a person would be hard pressed to find a house without half a dozen handguns and shotguns, or more, and a pickup truck without at least one handgun. The Connell ranch was no different. Inside was a Winchester target rifle weighing nearly twenty pounds and capable of hitting a deer square between the eyes at a thousand feet away, though a skilled hunter always aimed for the heart or lungs.

An expert marksman like Mr. Connell would attempt to "double lung" an animal—put two bullets in its lungs in rapid succession so that death would come to the animal quickly and humanely. Also in the Connell house was a standard pump-action buckshot rifle, a replica 1873 Long Colt single action, a 1911 Kimber double action, and an assortment of smaller handguns.

Joseph's older brother, Billy, and his father were avid hunters, shooting a dozen or more deer and their larger cousin, the elk, as well as an assortment of fowl life every year.

Of course, the animal being hunted determined whether they used buckshot shells (which at close range could go clear through a human being), birdshot (which would only burn a person mostly), or turkey load (pellets in between the size of the other two). Mr. Connell and Billy would skin the animals in the lower barn and let the carcass age for weeks before eating the meat.

Joseph had not been on a hunt in years. He used to love guns and he was a natural at shooting, even more than his older brother and father. But as he grew older and the crushing weight of his nightmares and visions took an ever-increasing toll on him, he couldn't stand the sights and sounds of death anymore.

The deafening echoing blast of death as a bullet pierced the animal's flesh was too much for him. He couldn't stomach watching his father or brother gut the dead beast and watch pools of blood pour out of its body cavity along with internal organs, staining the earth and grass. One day the shot of a 44-caliber Magnum handgun was so powerful that the sound of the blast slapped him in the face and he never touched a gun again.

An hour after waking from his nightmare Joseph walked down the stairs in a clean t-shirt and shorts and entered the kitchen, where his mother was still cleaning an already clean countertop, purely as an excuse to engage her son.

"Morning, Mom. What's for breakfast?" Joseph asked off-kilter, but trying to conceal that fact.

"It's three-thirty in the afternoon," Mrs. Connell replied.

Even for a Saturday, this was late in the day to be rising. Mrs. Connell knew from experience to tread lightly, because she had sensed more stress than usual lately in her baby son. Joseph took a glass from the counter, walked to the refrigerator for the bottle of orange juice, poured himself a glass, and then sat down at the kitchen table. He let out a long tired sigh and then took a drink from his glass.

As it was late spring, there were many chores to be done around the ranch. A creek crossing by the main barn was in need of repair. Corrals needed to be cleared of muck caused by the heavy May rains. Many fences needed painting. Gate hinges needed to be adjusted and lifted so they would close properly. Tin on the sides of the barns and grain sheds needed tightening after being loosened from gusting winds. Heavy yellow sulfur chloride blocks needed to be driven around the hills of the ranch for the cattle and horses to lick as mineral supplementation. But Mrs. Connell reminded Joseph of none of this.

"The horses could use some brushing to help them finish their slicking," she said. Slicking was the process of a horse shedding its thick winter coat of fur in favor of a thinner coat for the still arriving summer heat. Mrs. Connell sensed that Joseph could use a therapeutic task to soothe him. Joseph knew what his mother was not saying and doing and he appreciated it. He also knew that while some of the chores could wait, others should not.

"I'll get to that, Mom. But if it's okay with you, first I'd like to harness the yearlings," he said. A yearling was a horse that was one year old. At birth, a baby horse was a foal and rarely left its mare mother's side, whether suckling or otherwise learning by observing how to be a horse. At the age of six months, the foal was considered a weanling, which meant that it was taken from his its mother and corralled separately so that it could learn on its own how to properly act and survive within the horse herd hierarchy.

From the age of one to two years old, a horse was considered a yearling, meaning that it was old enough to be taught how to be handled by a human. By year three of life a horse was ready to be fully saddled and ridden.

Mrs. Connell turned and smiled toward her baby boy.

"If that's what you'd rather do Joey, that's okay with me. I've made some eggs, if you'd like?" she said.

Of all the natural foods found on a ranch, eggs were a treat. Whether it was the carrots, peas, onions, tomatoes, lettuce, or cabbage from Mrs. Connell's garden, to the beef, pork, or chicken grown on their free range pasture, food here in Montana had a vibrant quality that commercialized industrial agribusiness could never duplicate. Egg yolks from a factory, whose hen mothers were nourished only by factory gruel and a chemicalized life, were a pale yellow color.

When Mrs. Connell cracked open eggs from her hens, which had been free-range nourished not only on organic corn feed, but also from the extra protein content of grasshoppers and assorted insects to be found all around these hills, the egg yolks were a deep orange, bordering on red, bursting with nutrients and protein.

"Thanks, Mom. Eggs would be great," Joseph gratefully replied.

After Joseph finished his breakfast, he walked from the house down the gravel pathway to the main red barn that sat between the house and the horse corrals and fenced-in lots nearby. He filled a bucket full of oats and then made his way to the adjoining prairie grassland lot where half a dozen yearlings were a few hundred yards away at the far end of the fence, nibbling on nutritious improved pasture grass.

In a week or so it would be time to run these young ones up into the hills to strengthen their muscles, tendons, and ligaments. A young horse needed exercise or it would grow up weak and vulnerable to injury. But before Joseph could take care of that task, he had to get them harnessed, and that was why to harness these young horses he started by grabbing a bucket of tasty oats.

Joseph yelled to them, but he knew they were too inexperienced to respond. This was part of their conditioning. He yelled a second time, then walked close to them and poured a pile of oats on the ground. The smell of the oats was enough to get all the yearlings to wander over.

The sweetest grass in the world couldn't compare to the temptation of the aroma coming from the oats. It took only a minute for the yearlings to devour the small pile of oats Joseph had poured on the ground, so naturally they wanted the bounty he held in the bucket. As they walked over to him, Joseph walked back toward the corral where he needed them to be.

Even at this young age, each horse had its own distinctive personality, so while most simply and obediently followed Joseph back toward the corral, the alpha female of this yearling group (horses are a matriarchal society) pushed its way passed its fellow yearlings and attempted to eat immediately from Joseph's bucket. Just for good measure, hoping to get

Joseph to abandon the bucket, the yearling leaned into Joseph with its head and strong neck. It may have only been a yearling, but it was still over five hundred pounds of pure muscle and could stomp Joseph into the ground if it had really wanted to do so.

Fortunately for Joseph, horses were a herd animal of prey and it responded immediately to the determination of another (even a non-horse) to be the leader of the herd.

Joseph gave the pushy yearling a swift elbow in the neck. A horse's neck was way too muscular to cause even the slightest bit of pain, but it was a message clearly received by an animal that had been programmed through millions of years of evolution to avoid confrontation if possible, so the elbow did the trick—the oats would have to wait.

Once Joseph had walked the horses back into the corral that he needed them to be in, which adjoined the round pen he would use to train them to wear a halter, he closed the gate behind them and emptied the oats onto the ground.

This was the positive reinforcement loop he needed to teach them. If they obeyed him they got oats. If they didn't, they did not. One or two more times of this training and Joseph wouldn't even have to walk the few hundred yards to the other end of the lot and pour the small pile on the ground. Eventually, just hearing him yell for them would be enough to entice them to saunter back into the corral where he needed them—provided that every time they did there was a fresh pile of delicious oats waiting for them.

Growing horses such as these needed the extra nourishment that grasses alone could not optimally provide, so using a source of desired food as a leverage tool was a perfect pillar of horse training—and he knew these pillars like the back of his hand.

After giving each yearling enough time to finish eating the oats, Joseph approached the first horse nearest him, stood to its left flank, and gave it a gentle slap on its hind quarters—just enough to get it running in the direction he needed toward the round pen. Once he got the yearling inside the round pen, he closed the gate behind him. He reached for a halter that had an eight-foot rope attached to it and started walking toward the yearling. Instinctively the horse ran from him. As far as the horse knew, Joseph was a predator and coming to eat him. The fact that he had just fed it tasty oats was not enough to overcome millions of years of instinct as an animal of prey.

The round pen, which was either dirt or mud, depending on recent weather, was thirty feet in diameter with wooden walls ten feet high that formed a perfect circle. It allowed the horse to run itself tired without either getting away nor finding the safety of a corner, where it could hide and potentially hit Joseph with a lethal kick from its deadly hooves.

Joseph didn't mind that the horse ran from him. He just made sure, by twirling the halter in the air like a lasso, that it only ran in one direction. Consistency was key. Joseph simply walked behind the horse twirling the rope for as long as it took for the horse to tire itself out. It was simply a matter of proper stimulus training. Eventually the horse was tired enough to stop running in circles and look directly at Joseph, at which point Joseph stopped twirling the rope and stood still. The yearling was discovering that he was not a threat after all.

It didn't usually take Joseph very long for this exchange of non-verbal communication to occur, but if it did he had no choice but to see it through. If he ever quit before harnessing the yearling, he would only be guaranteeing that the next attempt would be even harder.

Once the yearling had stopped, Joseph slowly walked over to it and placed the rope halter around its head. This was the first step in desensitizing the animal to human contact and control. After placing the halter around the yearling's head, Joseph did not pull on the rope to coax it out of the round pen. He simply turned and walked away, letting the animal's herd instinct do the work for him.

Now that Joseph had been established as this yearling's leader, it chose to follow him out of the round pen and back to the holding corral, where he repeated the process until all six yearlings each had a halter around its head for the first time.

He moved on to the corral holding the dozen or so adult horses and groomed them with a soft bristled brush, as his mother had asked. She was right. It was as soothing to him as it was to the horse he was brushing. Joseph admired horses. They were well-equipped for survival. With their eyes placed on the sides of their heads, they had nearly a full three hundred and sixty degrees of vision. Their ears could turn independently of each other, depending on where the sound of a potential threat may be coming from.

At full size, a mare could be a thousand pounds of pure muscle, while a stallion could top twelve hundred pounds. Everyone in the Connell family knew of people who had lost fingers to a horse or had been severely injured when not respecting their boundaries and needs.

Joseph gave each horse all the respect it deserved and he was never in danger around them. Horses were extremely perceptive creatures and could read the non-verbal language of a human with piecing accuracy. They knew Joseph to be a pure person with no intentions of ill will and as such they sought out his company.

Joseph was almost finished brushing the last of the adult horses when the alpha female, Happy, a beautiful white mare with colorful brown patches on it, wandered back over for seconds. Happy nickered at Joseph that she wanted more, but he ignored her.

When that didn't work, she gently shoved him with her nose. Still, Joseph knew better than to give into this approach. If he did, he was setting himself up for a future filled with a thousand shoves of Happy's nose every time she wanted some extra grooming. Finally the insistent horse rested its head gently on Joseph's shoulder—a horse's way of saying, "please."

That got him.

"All right, Happy. Perhaps I didn't spend enough time brushing your Highness," Joseph said. He patted her belly and said, "You know, Happy, you're getting a serious case of hay belly. You get any fatter and I may have to put you on a diet."

Joseph was the only member of the family who could safely get away with patting a horse so firmly, square on the belly, especially the herd leader, and not worry about retribution. In fact, he was the only family member never to experience a horse pinning its ears to its head—the surest sign that a potentially painful bite from powerful equine incisor teeth was on the way.

Joseph loved horses. He loved to be around them. He loved their inherently regal nature. He loved the distinctive smell of horses—that unique mix of hay, earth, grass, equine sweat and body oil. He used to ride them endlessly as a younger boy, but now it had been years since he had saddled up.

He missed riding them and they missed being ridden by him. The worse his nightmares and visions became, the more he pulled away from all those around him. Even, his beloved horses.

After Joseph finished satisfying Happy's need for extra grooming, he made his way further down the hill to the loafing shed he had built himself from ponderosa pine trees he had cut down when he was twelve years old. A loafing shed was a three-sided wooden structure, usually about forty feet long, with a roof but no front wall.

They were scattered all over the Connell ranch so that horses and cattle could find shelter as needed from the snow, wind, or rain depending on the time of year. Joseph had built this one especially for his martial arts training and his fighting equipment, so that he would always have a sanctuary from a part of himself that he didn't understand.

The loafing shed was filled with a large, heavy kicking bag, a smaller bag for speed work, plus weights, pads, and homemade fighting equipment he had made himself. Besides the spear and short fighting sticks, the weapon he used the most was his handmade sword.

Since all of his homemade weapons were made of pine wood that he carved himself, he found himself on a fairly regular basis needing to replace them when a new technique he would attempt would end up smashing the wooden implement into splintered pieces. Joseph's only known coping mechanism to process the nightmare vision from the night before was to re-enact the battle by himself and see what he might have done differently or better.

While Joseph completed his sword work in the loafing shed, his older brother Billy pulled up to the Connell house in his mud-strewn, used pickup truck. At the age of just nineteen, he was his father's right-hand man in the family's bottling business. Billy could afford the fanciest pickup truck money could buy, but that would be disrespectful to his father, so he drove this old beater without complaint.

Billy had the same dark-brown colored hair that his mother and father did, in noticeable contrast to Joseph's lighter, almost beige-colored hair. Despite the difference in hair coloring, it was clear to anyone who saw them together that Joseph and Billy were brothers—they had the same high cheekbones, strong chin, green eyes, and both stood the same height.

As clear as it was that they were brothers, it was also impossible to miss the difference in countenance. Billy's expression was always relaxed and warm, while Joseph could never quite wipe clean the strain from his face, nor the creases around his eyes that were prematurely appearing on a boy of just seventeen. His eyes had a tired look that no boy his age should have.

Billy climbed the steps that led to the wrap-around porch of the Connell house. The entire house, as might be expected, was built from the ponderosa pine cut from these very foothill mountains. Billy had moved out of this house just one year ago when he married his high school sweetheart, Elizabeth.

He hadn't moved very far—just a mile down the road, but still well within the borders of the Connell family's twenty thousand acre ranch. Still, he missed living with his brother.

Billy took after his mother, and in more ways than hair coloring and temperament. He loved living in this part of Montana and did not care to spend time anywhere else. Sure, western Montana had beautiful mountains rising thousands of feet into the air, though Billy could see distant snow-capped mountain ranges even from their foothill home. Northern Montana had vast stretches of fertile plains that rolled for hundreds of miles, but this corner of the world was his home.

He especially loved spring time, when the yellowish green leaves of the cottonwood trees shimmered and danced when the wind blew, which it did often. Juniper trees, similar to the cedar tree, gave off a wonderful earthy smell. Growing usually only ten to fifteen feet or so off the ground, the juniper tree was nature's ladder fuel—when a forest became overgrown and needed to be cleared by nature's broom (a naturally occurring forest fire) it was the obedient juniper tree that caught fire first and transferred that fire to large neighboring trees so that nature could take its course.

The juniper tree also provided tasty berries that brought birds from far and wide. Springtime was well marked by the recurring sounds of nature—the distinctive chirping sound that each species of bird made, arriving at different intervals. First came the robin, then the Sandhill Crane. The meadowlark, with its deep yellow colored chest, was impossible to miss. When the Red-winged Blackbird arrived, Billy knew that winter was gone for good until the end of the next autumn season. Of course, the pleasant whinny from one horse to another was a sound every Connell family member enjoyed hearing.

The distinctive smells of spring were a natural joy, be it the potent scent of the ubiquitous sage brush or dozens of other plants native to these pastures, and when the rains finished they left behind a sharpened sense of smell of everything on the ranch.

The combination of aromas of plant life and the chirping of the birds revitalized a person's senses and spirit. Truly, life was abounding anew with fresh energy and vitality. Spring in Montana was bursting with new life, and Billy had his own contribution to add to the mix.

He walked into the kitchen to find his mother washing dishes that she had already washed four times. Repeating activities was her method of dealing with stress. Billy was about to tell his mother his good news, but the moment he looked into her eyes when she turned around to greet him, he knew something was wrong.

Mrs. Connell's older son seemed to come into this world nearly able to care for himself. He never even got into the kind of trouble a boy was expected to get into, so when Mrs. Connell learned at Joseph's birth that she was having another boy, she erroneously assumed that he would be just like his older brother. For a few years he was, and she was in Heaven with her two little angels. But when her youngest son, at five years old, started screaming about demons attacking him, she thought it was just a passing phase—a stage of fleeting nightmares he would quickly outgrow.

He did not.

From that age onward he withdrew slowly further and further from them.

Mrs. Connell reached into her apron and pulled out Joseph's blood stained t-shirt.

"I found this in Joey's room," she said.

As she spoke, the life seemed to drain out of her. "Third time this month," she continued.

Billy walked to his mother and took her in his arms, letting out a long, heavy-hearted sigh as he did.

"I'll talk to him, Mom," he said.

Mrs. Connell cried in her oldest son's arms, and not for the first time. But she quickly collected herself and returned to cleaning the dishes for a fifth time. Billy struggled with whether to share his good news with his mother at this moment, but decided to wait.

He walked out of his parent's house and down the hill toward Joseph's loafing shed. When he got close, he called to his baby brother.

"Joey!" he yelled.

Joseph stopped kicking the heavy bag and looked up to see his big brother, and his face softened with a genuine smile.

"Hey, what are you doing here?" he asked Billy.

"What, a guy needs a reason to come see his baby brother?" Billy replied.

Spending time with Billy was Joseph's favorite time of the day, any day.

"You are the only guy I know who would rather kick a bag than take a horse over those hills," Billy playfully jabbed.

"Horses kick back," Joseph replied, and smiled even more.

Joseph removed his practice equipment and he and Billy walked over to the nearest corral, where half a dozen horses were feeding on grass. It was dusk by now, which Billy always looked forward to—when the heat of the day gave way to a moist coolness and the breeze picked up and the yellowish hue of the sunlight was broken up by shadows from the nearby foothills as the sun began its retreat for the night.

They both rested their forearms on the top of the split-rail fence they had built with their father.

"So you graduate in two weeks, huh?" Billy asked.

"Three," Joseph replied.

"Dad's still hoping you'll come straight into the family business with us, you know, instead of heading off to college. We'll teach you everything you need to know better than any college," Billy offered.

"I can't live your life, Billy," Joseph replied.

Billy was stung, however unintentionally.

"God damn it, Joey! We're not exactly a bunch of hicks, you know?" Billy shot back.

"Sorry, that's not what I meant," Joseph whispered.

Billy recovered from his fleeting anger, born really of frustration. He had always felt it was his duty to look after his baby brother and he could not ignore his impotence at the task he had set for himself. But neither this fact nor his failure deterred him from his efforts.

"Remember that time we stole a hundred bottles from the plant and used them for target practice?" Billy asked.

"Remember? I've never seen Dad so mad then or since. I still don't know what he was madder about. Us shooting up a hundred perfectly good bottles or taking his shotgun without his permission," Joseph said.

"Do you remember what you said to the factory foreman? 'Shut up and give me the bottles. My Dad owns this place.' I swear if you were a foot taller he'd a hit you. And you were so scared you hid out in the meadow all night," Billy recounted.

Joseph laughed heartily.

"Yeah, that probably wasn't the smartest thing to say. I could tell he really wanted to swing at me too," Joseph said.

Billy loved seeing his brother laugh. It happened so rarely and was such a joy to behold. They lifted their arms off of the fence rail and began walking up the hill back toward the house.

"Well, little brother, tomorrow is your eighteenth birthday. You'll be a man. Couple of hours from now you won't be boy anymore. You can do whatever you want in life and whatever you choose, I'll support you," Billy said.

"Thanks, Billy," Joseph earnestly replied.

"Hey, Joey, guess what?" Billy asked.

"What?" Joseph replied.

"Elizabeth's pregnant," Billy said with a smile.

Joseph's face lit up at the news.

"We're naming him James," Billy said.

"How do you know it's gonna' be a boy?" Joseph asked.

"Joey, you know there hasn't been a girl born to the Connell family since medieval times because of the extra-high iron content in our blood," Billy replied.

Billy's statement elicited a deep belly laugh from Joseph.

"You couldn't even tell me what centuries the medieval times were. I don't know either, mind you, but that's simply the dumbest thing I ever heard," Joseph informed him.

"Yeah, well, you got a better explanation?" Billy asked.

"No, but I wouldn't mind having a girl someday," Joseph said.

"You?! Sorry to break it to you little brother, but you usually need a wife for such things, or a girlfriend at least, or a reasonable facsimile. You haven't even had anything resembling any of those things since... Hollie, and that was..." Billy said while trying to recall the year.

"Yeah, yeah, I know when that was, all I'm saying is..." Joseph said before Billy cut him off.

"Save it. When you're seventy and all alone and I've got grandkids, I don't want you blaming me," Billy said.

"I won't be alone," Joseph playfully protested.

"Come on, let's see what Mom's got for dinner," Billy replied.

Joseph stopped in his tracks. Billy took another two steps before realizing that Joseph was no longer beside him. He turned around to look at him.

"Can't. Got the tournament," Joseph said.

"Skip it, Joey. Elizabeth is on her way over. Have dinner with us, then…come to church," Billy said.

Joseph hadn't been to church since he was twelve years old. Mr. Connell did not cotton easily to his son refusing to attend church, but neither did he believe in forcing a growing boy into doing something he felt so powerfully strong about, so he let it be, and Mrs. Connell and Billy followed suit. That didn't mean that Billy wouldn't keep trying to get his baby brother back into the church-going habit. He thought maybe the opening of his news of Elizabeth's pregnancy might be just the opportunity.

"Can't," Joseph replied again.

"Okay, Joey," Billy responded in defeat.

Chapter 2

Two hours later Joseph stood alone amongst hundreds of competitors dressed in martial arts uniforms. They were of assorted rank, from the lowest beginner white belt to the highest ranking black belt. Some wore white uniforms and some wore black uniforms, depending on which martial arts school they belonged to and what historical custom each style required color wise.

Joseph did not have on a uniform, nor a belt of a specific color designating his rank within that particular school. He stood in an old t-shirt and even older sweat pants, yet he was legendary throughout this part of Montana and word of his abilities had spread throughout the state.

Since the age of fifteen, Joseph had been competing in the adult division, which normally required a minimum age of eighteen. The problem was that Joseph was so formidable that youth competitors were dropping out of the tournaments, knowing they couldn't defeat him. This was costing the governing body much needed revenue in the form of lost competition fees.

Joseph didn't mind moving up to fight the adult men. He knew that not one of them could ever come close to the battles he had fought elsewhere.

Since Joseph had moved up to the adult division, he had been a boon to the elders who ran the martial arts organization in these parts because people came from far and wide to see him. Some came to compete against him—always they left in defeat. Some came to watch the boy wonder out strike all comers, even on the rare occasion when the highest ranking teacher of a particular school would test his mettle against him.

Joseph didn't care about the victories nor the trophies. He sought out no one to engage before or after each competition, though he was not aloof if anyone approached him. He could have had well over one hundred trophies back in his room if he wanted, but not one ever made its way back home with him—he kept not one of them.

Trophies were not why he fought. It was the only coping mechanism he could come up with, but with the recent rise in onslaught severity, he wasn't sure how much longer even this would prove useful.

Joseph waited patiently to start his championship match against his thirty-year-old competitor, Tom. Joseph had never seen him fight before, nor heard of him, but Tom was also undefeated and had traveled from as far away as Colorado to test his talent against this phenom. He stood an impressive six-foot, six-inches tall and towered over Joseph. Tom's longer limbs would give him a distinct advantage when it came to reach, but Joseph was unperturbed.

Tom was still a good half a foot shorter than the attackers he was accustomed to fighting.

Though this was the championship match Joseph waited to compete in, this was still a fairly no-frills organization, so the championship ring consisted of merely a fifteen-foot square on the convention floor marked off with thick black tape. An assortment of competitors in their martial arts uniforms formed the crowd nearest to the square, while hundreds of people sat in the stands.

While Tom consulted in the opposite corner with his instructor, Joseph stood alone. The bout couldn't begin until the announcer arrived, as well as until the five judges made their way to the square. The contest would be judged by four junior judges and one senior judge, who was also the referee for the fight. They had all been fighters in their day, but now were well beyond competing age.

As Joseph stood alone, a soft-spoken sixteen year-old high school boy by the name of Mike, dressed in his white martial arts uniform and black belt, approached Joseph. They knew each other from school and around town. They were not friends, though not because of any shortcoming nor defect in Mike. Joseph simply did not have any friends.

"Joe, can I ask you something?" Mike inquired.

Joseph had no special preparation to complete as Tom did, so he didn't mind Mike approaching him so close to the fight.

"Sure, Mike. What's up?" Joseph replied.

Not far away, concealed by the crowd and out of Joseph's field of vision, stood Lahiri.

He was from India and though his country was known from antiquity through the modern day for producing the finest fabrics—cotton, silk, and others- in an endless variety of vibrant colors—he was dressed in a simple brown cloth garment he had made himself, spun on a handloom made of wood that he had built. While Lahiri had originally stood a modest five-foot, eight-inches tall, he had been shrunken by time, and now stood a more diminutive five-foot, five-inches tall.

While there was a time when he possessed a head full of thick, jet-black hair, he had long since outlived the life cycle of human head hair; but no matter, for his bald head only added to his quiet presence of dignity and humble grace.

He listened intently to Joseph's conversation.

"I was just wondering, um, I was just wondering, I'm fighting later tonight for the junior title, and, um, I was wondering if you had any advice for me?" Mike asked Joseph.

"Sure, Mike. You're fighting against Fred. He's tough," Joseph said.

"Tell me about it," Mike replied.

"You want to take Fred out?" Joseph asked.

"Very much," Mike eagerly replied.

"He's got a hard left jab and a wicked right hook. Almost beat me once when we were ten years old," Joseph said.

"Yeah, he still talks about that time too," Mike added.

"You stay out of his danger zone and hit him from a safe distance with a left roundhouse kick, he'll go down like a sack a' potatoes," Joseph said.

"But, but I can't, my left hamstring is hurt," Mike protested.

Lahiri listened intently as Joseph spoke.

"I know it is, Mike. So does Fred and probably so does everyone else here today. You've been favoring it walking around all day long. How could anyone miss it?" Joseph asked.

"But if I try that I could tear my hamstring," Mike said fearfully.

"Probably real bad too, Mike. You might even need surgery afterwards. But do you want to limp out of here in defeat or maybe get carried out of here in victory? I'm not telling you what to do. But if you want to win...it needs to be done," Joseph imparted.

Mike nodded his head. "Thanks, Joe, " he said.

"No problem, Mike. Good luck," Joseph said as Mike walked away favoring his, for the moment, only slightly injured left hamstring muscle.

Lahiri noticed the judges and announcer making their way toward the championship square, so he discreetly made his way into the stands nearby.

The announcer walked to the center of the square and raised his microphone to address the crowd. As the announcer enthusiastically introduced first Tom, and then Joseph, the crowd roared with applause and foot stomping. Joseph did not respond as Tom did with hand waving and fist pumping. He simply stood and waited for the match to begin.

The head referee walked to the center of the square as each of the four junior judges made their way to each of the four corners of the square. Joseph and Tom, both barefoot, each walked to the center and faced each other as the head referee went over the rules.

"Okay, fellas, you know the rules but let's review 'em anyway. No eye gouges, shots to the groin, throat, or kneecaps. Obey my commands at all times. Got that?" he asked.

Both Joseph and Tom nodded that they did. The head judge stepped back, yelled, "Fight!" and the championship match had begun.

Lahiri watched, concerned for Joseph.

Joseph and Tom stalked each other around the square, neither ready to commit at first, like big-game cats stalking each other as prey. Suddenly in a flash, Tom surprised Joseph with a lightning fast axe kick—smashing his heel down onto Joseph's forehead from overhead. Joseph was catapulted off his feet and back into the fighters that surrounded the square.

The crowd was deafeningly loud in their reaction. No one had ever hit Joseph so cleanly or so hard.

"Holy shit!" Mike exclaimed from the sidelines.

A large welt immediately formed on Joseph's forehead as he shook off the momentary dementia. He had a significant concussion from his brain getting slammed into the front of his skull as his head snapped back at a dangerously fast speed, but he would never admit it. The fighters helped Joseph to his feet as the head judge walked over to a dazed Joseph. The head judge motioned for the fight doctor to come over and inspect Joseph's injury.

"Looks pretty bad to me, kid. You want me to stop this?" the fight doctor asked.

Joseph shook his head no. The head judge leaned over to Joseph.

"Son, you get hit by another one of those and I'm stoppin' this fight. I don't care if you are the undefeated champ. You got that?" he whispered in Joseph's ear.

Joseph nodded that he understood.

Both Joseph and Tom stood in the center of the square as all five judges raised their left hands in the air, awarding the obvious point to Tom. The head judge motioned to resume the fight. Joseph was much more cautious as he approached Tom. A series of bone crushing knees, elbows, kicks, and stinging palm slaps were exchanged repeatedly, but Joseph would not be done in so easily, and neither could Tom's defenses be penetrated.

Lahiri's look of concern grew more pronounced.

Every person in the building, except Lahiri, was on their feet. They knew they were seeing something never before witnessed. Even the younger fighters who would be competing later stood mesmerized.

Joseph initiated a left roundhouse kick, hoping to end this fight with one clean blow, but Tom was faster, and responded with his own devastating left round-house kick, and caught Joseph squarely in the ribs, breaking several of them, a most painful injury where the necessary act of breathing becomes the source of pain, with the expanding diaphragm muscle forcing broken pieces of rib to move out of its way so that life-giving lungs can expand and fill with oxygen.

Joseph involuntarily collapsed to the floor. The crowd went wild in disbelief as the head judge declared Tom the winner, not even waiting for the doctor's official declaration. The head judge then helped the fight doctor get Joseph to his feet, as Tom was instantly mobbed by fellow fighters for his victory. Everyone liked Joseph, they just couldn't believe that they had actually seen him defeated, and so convincingly, and many wanted a part of Tom's moment of glory.

Within minutes Joseph sat alone in the locker room on a wooden bench, except for the fight doctor who finished examining his broken ribs.

"I'm pretty sure that whole right side is broken. X-ray would tell us for certain. Really nothing to do but let them heal. I can wrap them if you'd like," the fight doctor offered to Joseph.

Outside in the woods a deer sat resting on the ground.

It was a male buck deer. A typical buck deer in this part of Montana could grow to a maximum of two hundred and fifty pounds, but this was no typical deer. It weighed in at over a thousand pounds of sinew and muscle. A typical buck deer might have antlers four to five feet long. This deer's regal thicket of antlers stretched out over ten feet in length. This particular deer did not partake in the customary habits of its brethren. It did not consume food for nourishment, mark its territory, nor make any efforts to procreate.

It waited.

"No, thanks, Doc. I'll be fine," Joseph replied.

With that the fight doctor gathered up his supplies, put them back in his black bag, and started to walk out. He stopped for a moment and turned around to say something to Joseph.

"You were bound to lose eventually, son. You're still one hell of a fighter. Sometimes it's just your time," he offered.

"Thanks, Doc," Joseph gratefully whispered.

The fight doctor turned and exited the locker room. Joseph sat alone for a moment to collect his thoughts before gingerly reaching out to collect his gloves and tape and put them in his duffle bag. He moved slowly to avoid the shooting pain that hit him if he moved too abruptly.

After several moments Lahiri entered the locker room, unnoticed by Joseph. His steps were absent of noise, as if he displaced nothing as he moved through the world around him.

In the woods the massive deer suddenly rose to its feet. It blinked several times.

Lahiri stared at a pink, jagged-shaped birthmark on Joseph's solar plexus, at the top of his abdomen. For a moment Lahiri seemed to not notice Joseph at all, just the pink, jagged-shaped birthmark. Joseph looked up and saw Lahiri standing there.

"Hi," Joseph offered softly.

"Hello," Lahiri replied.

The deer blinked rapidly several times again and focused its attention.

"I believe I could be of some assistance," Lahiri offered.

Still in great pain, but respectful of this unknown man's gesture of goodwill, Joseph whispered, "No, thank you. A little ice and I'll be okay."

He returned his attention to placing his remaining belongings in his duffle bag. Lahiri stood in the doorway to the locker room and watched him. Joseph looked up at Lahiri and gave him a genuine smile, then returned his attention to his duffle bag.

Finally, Lahiri turned to leave, but not before looking one more time at the birthmark on Joseph's abdomen.

As Lahiri exited the locker room, the massive deer in the woods dug its oversized hooves into the earth below with purpose and took off running at full speed through the woods.

Minutes later Joseph had made his way into his pickup truck and was driving, carefully, back home. As he drove through the woods, his entire family—his father, his mother, Billy, and pregnant Elizabeth— sat in church singing hymns along with the rest of the full congregation. As the hymn finished, the priest stood and walked to the alter to tend to his flock.

"In response to Job's plea that he be allowed to see God and hear from him the cause of his suffering, God answers, not by justifying his actions before man, but by referring to his omniscience and almighty power," the priest said.

Back in the woods the deer continued its full bore race through the trees.

As Joseph drove fifty miles per hour, even though the posted speed limit was sixty-five miles per hour, he approached a gentle bend in the road. As he came around the other side of the bend, the deer jumped from the woods out onto the road and waited for him.

Joseph barely reacted.

He was in too much pain to notice that this deer was no earthly size. He assumed from a distance that it was an elk and he had been in this situation a thousand times before. He reflexively flashed his high beam lights on and off several times, sure that it would scare the animal harmlessly away.

It did not.

Within moments Joseph could see that the animal in his path was inexplicably not going to move. In a fraction of a second, Joseph's world-class reflexes were marshaled for battle and he was instantly in a hyper-primitive state of being. His conscious mind, incapable of providing any meaningful contribution in this critical moment, was shunted aside as nerve cells along his spinal column mobilized the forces of survival.

In a millisecond, vast amounts of adrenaline were squeezed from the tiny walnut-shaped adrenal glands sitting atop his kidneys, flooding his bloodstream. His heart raced, at an otherwise lethal speed, forcing blood from his internal organs and driving it into his extremities, gorging the muscles of his arms and legs in an effort to avert this almost certain date with death.

Joseph's body stopped sending pain signals from his broken ribs as his right foot slammed down onto the brake pedal. His foot smashed clean through the floorboard of the old pickup truck. As white smoke poured from underneath the tires screeching atop the pavement, Joseph swerved his truck to the right to avoid hitting the animal.

It was to no avail.

The deer mirrored his actions. Joseph swerved his truck to the left. The deer matched him move for move.

The distance between them shrank to nothing as the deer lowered its head and massive antlers into its certain death as the grill of Joseph's truck crashed directly into it. Joseph realized at the final moment that it was not an elk, but that it was a deer the likes of which he had never seen before.

The deer had shifted its head to its left on impact, causing the truck to career off the road to Joseph's right. His truck flew at full speed into a massive tree, sending him careening through the windshield, as the mortally wounded deer rolled into a ditch on the far side of the road.

As Joseph flew through the windshield, shards of jagged, flying glass cut into his face and metal violently crunched all around him. His now disfigured face smashed into the thick trunk of the massive tree as blood spurted from his gashed mouth and he fell to the ground, near death.

Joseph lay motionless on the ground as his family began to sing another hymn in church.

Steam spewed from the smashed radiator of the truck's engine as Lahiri stepped out from the trees. He had watched the entire horrific event unfold. He calmly walked past the dead deer to the motionless Joseph lying on the ground, whose body was mangled and bloody. His blood, that just a moment ago was nourishing his tissues, was now drowning them from within.

Lahiri knelt gently next to Joseph, raised his blood stained t-shirt, and touched the pink, jagged-shaped birthmark on Joseph's solar plexus. Joseph wasn't breathing and would not be long for this world.

Lahiri did nothing for a moment, then he let go of Joseph's blood soaked t-shirt and affectionately caressed his bloody forehead. Joseph had moments at most to live. Finally, Lahiri placed his left hand over Joseph's heart and his right hand over Joseph's nose and mouth. He closed his eyes and concentrated.

Birds chirped nearby.

A second later, Lahiri's hands began to glow with small illuminations of white light. Suddenly the blood that was profusely pouring from Joseph's mouth, nose, eyes, and ears ceased its determined flow.

Lahiri removed his hands from Joseph's broken body and reached into Joseph's pocket and pulled out his cell phone. He dialed 911, waited for an operator to answer, then spoke softly.

"Please send an ambulance to Wicker Road, just north of Stables Lane. There has been a most terrible accident and a boy is badly hurt," he said into the phone.

He then closed the phone, dropped it to the ground near Joseph's body, caressed his blood stained forehead one more time, then walked silently back into the woods.

Chapter 3

The waiting room of the hospital was small, with only enough chairs for a dozen or so people. While there were other people besides the Connell family present, waiting for loved ones to be treated, none were nearly as gruesomely injured as the Connell's family member. Out of a spontaneous sense of respect, those other people gave Mr. and Mrs. Connell, Billy, and his pregnant wife Elizabeth a wide berth, as if to give them extra room to breathe and grieve.

Mrs. Connell sobbed as Mr. Connell held his wife of over twenty beautiful years and comforted her as best he could. Billy was speechless nearly to the point of being numb as he stared off into space, yet still he held Elizabeth's hand.

A doctor dressed in scrubs and drenched in sweat approached the Connell family and removed his surgical cap from his head as he spoke—an involuntary gesture of respect.

"Mr. and Mrs. Connell, I'm Dr. Musser, Joseph's neurosurgeon," he said.

Mrs. Connell rose immediately, as did the rest of Joseph's grief stricken family.

"How is he?" she asked pleadingly.

"We were able to repair the damage to his internal organs as well as can be expected," Dr. Musser replied.

"Oh, dear God," Mrs. Connell cried.

"There is massive swelling in his brain and his neck is broken. We have removed the back portion of his skull temporarily to relieve the pressure on his brain. Nevertheless, he has slipped into a coma," Dr. Musser continued.

"For how long?" Mr. Connell asked.

"Mr. Connell, there is no way to know, but I have to be honest with you. I have no medical explanation for why your son is still alive. His ruptured aorta alone should have killed him at the scene. There is so much damage to so many internal organs, I'm sorry, I don't mean to be disrespectful. I just mean to say that…you might want to say your goodbyes while you still have a chance. I'll take you to him," Dr. Musser offered.

Dr. Musser led the stunned Connell family over to Joseph's room, then waited outside as they entered with equal parts fear and faith that battled for control of their badly battered emotions. The assorted machines keeping him alive had a macabre rhythm. They were unmistakably the sounds of life, but also seemed to be reminding the visitors that he was alive, but not by much.

Most of Joseph's face was held together by opaque sutures. His jaw and nose were shattered and his eyes grotesquely swollen shut. He looked far more dead than alive. There was a synthetic plastic fiber guard covering the back of his head, where the portion of his skull had been removed. The metal halo, with spikes drilled directly into his skull, kept his head from shifting on his broken neck.

Mrs. Connell reached out to touch her baby boy, but with her fingertips inches from his face, she stopped, for fear of causing more damage. She broke down crying as she pulled her hand back toward her body.

Billy cried quietly as he hugged Elizabeth. Mr. Connell, powerless to do any more than his oldest son, hugged his broken-hearted wife.

Chapter 4

Joseph did inexplicably survive the night and some months after his doctor had reasonably given him up for dead, the many scars that outlined his once handsome face seemed even to fade a bit, but still there was no response. He was medically designated as being in a vegetative state, with no reasonable expectation of ever regaining consciousness, but this did not deter his family in the slightest.

On this particular day, his doting older brother, Billy, sat alone by his bed, holding his baby brother's hand and rubbing it, as much for his own comfort as for Joseph's.

"Come on, Joey. I've seen you take worse shots than this," Billy said to him. "Remember that time when you were thirteen and you got a crew cut, and one of the Hackett boys said you looked like a beaver's butt, so you decked him? When Dave got up off the ground he was so mad, I thought his first punch was going to split your head right open. But before I can jump in to help, half of them are layin' on the ground cryin' and the other half are too scared to fight."

Billy smiled as he looked at his baby brother, half expecting a response. None was forthcoming. He rested his weary head on Joseph's hospital bed and thought some more about that moment he wished he could get back.

At six months after the accident, still there was no response. Joseph lay motionless, but very much still alive. The life support system had been removed and he was breathing on his own, much to the shock of the medical team assigned to his case.

On this lonely night, his mother and father kept him company, steadfastly refusing to believe that he was unaware of their presence, even if he couldn't let them know it. Mrs. Connell read from her Bible as she sat by the side of his bed. The room was dark except for the reading light she sat under. Mr. Connell sat nearby—a saddened silhouette in the darkness.

"'If the flesh came into being because of the Spirit, it is a wonder. But if the Spirit came into Being because of the flesh, it is a wonder of wonders. Indeed, I am amazed at how this great wealth made its home in this poverty,'" she recited.

Mrs. Connell closed the book and cried quietly, leaning back in her chair, taking her out of the light as Mr. Connell leaned forward, out of the darkness.

"You've got to come out of this soon, Joey. Fall's almost over. All the work we need to get done's going to be harder once winter hits. But either way, we'll... we'll..." he stammered over his words.

A nurse gently pushed open the door to Joseph's hospital room to deliver a message.

As the door slowly opened in the world without, *Joseph continued his battle in his world within.*

Blood spewed from his mouth as he knelt in pain on the ground.

Seconds passed.

The three warriors hovered over the fallen Joseph, their swords ready.

More seconds passed.

Still the warriors did not move.

As the nerve cells throughout his body recovered and came back online, Joseph fought back the pain that had momentarily incapacitated him. Suddenly, anger and determination supplanted fear and anguish. Having never let go his sword, he tightened his grip, and still on his knees, swung his sword overhead at the first warrior nearest to him. The man retreated out of range, just barely.

As Joseph rose to one knee the second warrior swung his sword down with sudden fury, but Joseph deflected the attack as he rose to his feet and counter-attacked with venom of his own. In a loud clash of metal his enemy defended his onslaught, but was knocked backwards. Joseph spun into a back kick and caught the third warrior in the stomach hard, sending him careening backwards.

Joseph returned his attack to the first warrior and faked a high attack, then cut low and severed the man's legs at his knees. He turned without pause to the second warrior, oblivious to the blood that had splattered on him, and lunged at the man, smacking him in the face with the handle portion of his sword—killing him instantly.

Now it was one on one. Joseph's rage grew with his determination to break free. With his sights locked on the lone remaining warrior's unprotected neck, Joseph swung his sword with all the speed and strength he could muster. The warrior leaned backwards, but not far enough, as Joseph's sword cut through the man's jugular vein in his neck.

As the mortally wounded warrior collapsed to the ground, soaked in his own blood, Joseph's brief expectation of freedom was unexpectedly interrupted.

In the dark night of black gloom and full moon, instantly a statue of four lions appeared, perched atop a cylindrical pillar. Just as the three now dead warriors were all clones of each other, so too were these four lions identical in every detail.

Joseph's chest heaved in strained breath as he took in the sight. The four lions stood back to back to one

another, so that they each faced one of the four direc-
tions. They appeared to be no earthly representations
of lions in more ways than one. The thick mane of
each wrapped not only around their head and chin,
but also down their front in thick, curly strands.

They were twice the size of any mortal lion. Around
the outside of the pillar atop which they stood were
images of a wheel with twenty-four spokes, under
each lion. Between the first two wheels was an image
of an elephant. Between the second and third wheels
was a galloping horse. Between the third and fourth
wheels was a bull. Between the fourth wheel and the
first was another lion.

Just as Joseph finished visually digesting this new
sight and tried to make sense of what it meant, his
quest for meaning was quickly rendered moot, as the
lions sprang to life and charged at him with swarming
intensity.

Paralyzed with fear, Joseph dropped his sword
where he stood and could make no move to flee. The
lions continued their charge without regard for the
corpses underfoot. Joseph knew death was charging at
him with razor sharp fangs ready to shred him before
he could raise a hand to defend himself.

Back in the world without, the nurse who entered
Joseph's hospital room whispered, "Mr. Connell,
there's a call for you. It's your son, Billy."

"Take a message, please," Mr. Connell replied.

"He said it's urgent," the nurse informed him.

Mr. Connell stood from his chair and walked to the nurse's station.

Back in the world within, the four lions continued their charge at the helpless Joseph. The leader of the lion ran faster than the other three and leaped at full speed through the air, growling with deafening violence as it landed atop Joseph, knocking him to the ground as it enveloped him. As Joseph was brutally slammed to the earth below under the lion's heavy weight, he had the wind knocked out of him. The lion leader draped its massive paws astride Joseph's shoulders, preventing him from moving, barely leaving him able to breath.

He cried out, "I want to..."

Joseph's mother was clasping at her Bible when the silence in Joseph's hospital room was suddenly and unexpectedly broken.

"Go home," he whispered.

Mrs. Connell's eyes opened wide. She jumped from her chair, threw open the door to his room, and screamed incredulously into the hallway while gasping for air, "John! John! He's awake! He's awake!"

Chapter 5

One year later, Joseph was indeed more than awake. It was a brisk autumn day and the grass meadows had all turned brown, though they still held nutritional value for the horses that grazed upon them in their corrals.

Billy stood not far from the fence as he caught a football thrown hard by Joseph.

"Hey, not so hard," Billy playfully yelled as he threw the ball softly back to Joseph.

Joseph caught the football with his left hand and guided it down to his lap, using the side of his wheelchair for leverage. He placed his fingers over the laces, working to get a tight enough grip to raise the ball to throw it back to Billy. His legs rested off to his right side—unusable. His right arm and hand, limp and lifeless like his legs, rested on the seat of his wheelchair.

Even covered in heavy clothing, his legs and right arm were emaciated, with little muscle tissue left in appearance to separate skin from bone.

Joseph threw the ball back to Billy, but several feet over Billy's head, forcing him to turn around and run after the ball.

"You did that on purpose," Billy accused, feigning protest over having to chase the ball.

He ran to pick it up, but when he turned back around he saw that Joseph had wheeled himself away, closer to the barn. He walked over and stopped a few feet behind him.

"Joey?" Billy asked.

Joseph struggled to stay in control.

"I want to go back," he whispered.

Billy approached closer and knelt beside him.

Joseph was near tears. The passage of a year had done nothing to soothe him.

"I wish...I wish I was five years old again...before they started. I keep thinking it can't be true," he said.

He made no effort to stop the tears from streaming down his face. Billy had never seen his little brother cry. Not even when they were kids.

"Sometimes I forget. I'm running or kicking, but then...but then, I wake up, and my mind clears, and I remember," he sobbed.

Billy moved in closer, on Joseph's left side, kneeling beside the armrest to Joseph's wheelchair.

"Joey, you've got to get past this. Accept it and, and live your life," Billy offered.

Joseph protested from the depths of despair, his spirit in ruins but not quite as badly broken as his body. He reflexively reached out with his only good limb and pushed Billy away from him, knocking him to the ground.

Billy lay on the cold ground for a moment, too stunned to notice the stinging pain in his jaw and mouth. With Joseph crying, his mouth agape but no sound, Billy recovered and rose to his knees. He lowered the armrest to Joseph's wheelchair and took his forlorn brother in his arms for the first time in a very long time.

Joseph's head collapsed onto his older brother's shoulder. Tears streamed down his teenaged face. Billy cradled him and rocked him gently.

"It's okay, little brother. It's okay," he whispered.

Several days later, Joseph was alone in the house. It was midday, so his father and brother were at work and his mother was in town shopping for household supplies. Using the electric power knob he made his way from the kitchen into the family room. All of the door jams throughout the house had been recut, made large enough for his wheelchair to fit through so that moving from room to room would not be a problem.

Mr. Connell and Billy built the ramp that led from the front of the property up to the wrap-around porch. Several interior walls had to be moved so that an electric chairlift could be installed, which enabled Joseph to move freely from the downstairs of the house to his room upstairs.

Fortunately, the upstairs bathroom was wide enough to accommodate his wheelchair, so other than adding horizontal and vertical metal grab bars on the wall and building a widened custom door, nothing more was needed construction-wise to accommodate him.

Upon reaching the end table near the couch, Joseph reached for the television remote control and turned it on. A reporter was in the middle of a segment.

"Amazingly enough, there are doctors willing to confirm that Kevin Talmide is pumping his blood solely with the power of his mind," said the reporter.

The television program cut to a pre-recorded segment of a man in his mid-thirties who was seated in a wheelchair, being pushed through a supermarket, as the reporter's voice was still heard.

"A full quadriplegic from birth, Kevin had been forced to spend his life on his back, since sitting in the upright position would cause his blood to pool in his feet, causing him to pass out," the reporter said.

Joseph's attention was firmly glued to the television program.

"At the root of all of this is something referred to as 'cosmic consciousness'. No one is exactly sure how to describe it, but it is supposed to be the highest form of enlightenment, where some claim the power of mind over matter is possible," the reporter continued.

The television show returned to a segment of the reporter speaking.

"I asked Kevin's long-standing physician what he thinks the cause of Kevin's amazing breakthrough is," the reporter said.

The program cut to a taped segment of the reporter interviewing Kevin's doctor.

"Now, Doctor, you did not teach Kevin this technique, is that correct?" asked the reporter.

"That is correct. Someone else did," replied the doctor.

"Can you tell us what has taken place here?" the reporter asked.

"I would say some of the nerve endings along his spinal column have found a way to reroute over the years, or come back online so to speak. Beyond that, I do not know. The mind is a powerful organ we do not fully understand," the doctor said.

"When you say 'mind', Doctor, by that you mean the brain?" asked the reporter.

"That is correct," replied the doctor.

"Isn't it true, Doctor, that we use only ten percent of our brain capacity?" asked the reporter.

"No, actually that's just a baseless urban legend. It has been proven through the use of CAT scans and

MRI technology that we use one hundred percent of our brain capacity," corrected the doctor.

"Well then, Doctor, isn't it possible that we do not use the full extent of our brain's capacity? What if our brain is like a million dollar Ferrari, that is currently only being driven at twenty miles per hour, when in fact with some more gas, or in this case, more training of the brain, that it could go more like two hundred miles per hour?" asked the reporter.

"I don't know how to answer a question like that," the doctor replied.

The program cut back to just the reporter.

"I also spoke with Dr. Patel, the man who taught Kevin this life altering technique. He is not only a respected psychiatrist from India who just arrived in this country two months ago, but he is also the author of several bestselling books on the mind/body connection," the reporter said.

The program cut to a segment of the reporter interviewing Dr. Patel, a genial, older gentleman with a pleasant paternal demeanor.

"Dr. Patel, can you explain this mind over matter phenomenon?" the reporter asked him.

"Well, I can try," replied Dr. Patel. "You see, if you touch your arm, you feel matter. If you feel a desire or emotion, that is energy. Science tells us that energy and matter are merely different forms of the same thing, the same essence, just as ice, water, and steam are different forms of hydrogen and oxygen, even though ice is very hard, water is very fluid, and steam is very light. From a western point of view, cosmic consciousness could be described as taking conscious control over otherwise involuntary bodily functions. From the point of view of my ancestors, it would be described as changing the nature of those involuntary functions to make them follow your voluntary commands," said Dr. Patel.

"So what you're saying, Dr. Patel, is that there really is no difference between our minds, and the matter of the universe?" asked the reporter.

"At a deeper level of reality, that is correct. But that is a very, very deep level of reality. I would say that in the case of Kevin Talmide, at the very least, he has taken conscious control of his blood pressure, raising it sufficiently to cause enough increase in flow to enable him to sit up," said Dr. Patel.

The program cut to a segment shot in India as the reporter spoke.

"An affiliate of ours in India was able to locate and interview one of that country's eminent yogis, those reclusive sages in the remote Himalayas alleged to possess these powers of mind over matter," said the reporter.

As Joseph watched with unbridled intensity, the program cut to a tape of a local Indian reporter and an interpreter as they made their way down a small hill. Off in the distance stood a smiling sage with long, wild hair, dressed in an orange robe, which to him signified purity. When they reached the sage, the interpreter conversed with him in Hindi, the main language of India. After a friendly exchange, the interpreter turned to the reporter and said, "He says you may ask him whatever you like."

"What exactly is cosmic consciousness?" asked the reporter.

The interpreter relayed the question.

The elderly smiling sage ruminated for a moment before answering the interpreter, who upon hearing the answer, replied to the reporter in English, "He says, 'How do you tell a sleeping man what it is like to be awake? He must awake and discover for himself.'"

The reporter had another question.

"Do you think the West could benefit from some of these cosmic consciousness practices?" asked the reporter.

The interpreter again relayed the question to the old man and then relayed his response.

"He says, 'Thinking will get you nowhere,'" said the interpreter.

The program returned to the original reporter.

"Is this the next big step in the growing movement toward alternative healing? Is this the long awaited crossroads where science and religion finally converge? This is Harry Thompson for this edition of 'The New Millennium,'" said the reporter.

A dozen phone calls and an hour later, Joseph was still on the phone in the family room.

"But Dr. Patel," he pleaded, "If you can teach Kevin to move his blood with the power of the mind, you can teach me to move my arm and legs."

"Joseph," Dr. Patel replied, "There is a world of difference between the biofeedback technique of raising one's blood pressure enough to permit sitting upright, and getting paralyzed limbs to move by having neurotransmitters jump across nerve synapses that have been severed. It may seem like a tiny distance to you, but to the neurotransmitters it is a distance further apart than the opposite sides of the Grand Canyon."

"It's possible, Dr. Patel. It's possible. I know it is," Joseph begged.

Dr. Patel sighed.

"What you are asking is possible, Joseph. I heard of such things very often when I was a boy growing up in India. But I cannot give it to you. However, I do know someone who might be able to. He came to visit me about a year ago, but he is quite far away now. I would be happy to give you his address," Dr. Patel said.

Later that night Joseph sat in his wheelchair in his room watching his television. Playing on it was a tape of him at a karate tournament, performing a kata—a dance of karate moves simulating a fight.

His performance was majestic and graceful, sharp and beautiful. After a few moments there was a knock at his door. He turned the power to the television off and the screen went blank.

"Come on in," Joseph yelled.

Billy entered his bedroom and looked at the blank television Joseph was sitting in front of. He noticed the remote control in his hand.

"Good show?" Billy tried to joke.

"I was just looking at stuff," Joseph replied quietly.

"Yeah," Billy replied.

"What's up, Billy?" Joseph asked.

"Dad's still hoping you'll come work with us at the plant. He even had an engineer install a special elevator that leads right to your office," Billy said.

"Like a mole that never leaves its tunnel," Joseph replied.

"Joey, you know that's not true," Billy answered.

Joseph took a slow, labored breath as his mood now saddened.

"That God-damn deer just wouldn't move. It was unreal. If I told you how big it was, I swear, you wouldn't believe me," Joseph said.

His throat tensed and tightened, restricting his breathing.

"The ambulance and road crews couldn't find it," Bill said softly. "They said it must have limped away and died off in the woods somewhere."

"You know how on those cable medical shows, when the victim wakes up and doesn't remember anything? You want to know the last thing I remember," Joseph asked.

Billy stared silently at his little brother.

"The last thing I remember was the crack of my neck breaking when my face hit that tree. It was the loudest sound I ever heard…I don't know why some people are cursed," he said.

"Joey, you're not…" Billy tried to say, but his eyes moistened with emotion and he couldn't finish the lie.

Joseph wiped a rogue tear from the corner of his left eye.

"I have to leave this place," Joseph said.

"What do you mean, 'leave this place'? This is your home. Leave and go where?" Billy asked.

"I don't know. I…don't…know," Joseph replied.

Billy stared at Joseph, his concern growing by the moment. Joseph looked away, unable to speak any further. After a moment Billy silently turned and walked out of Joseph's room, quietly closing the door behind him.

As he made his way downstairs and toward the front door, he saw his parents in the kitchen.

"Night, Mom. Night, Dad," he said as he made his way closer to the door.

Mrs. Connell smiled at her oldest son. Mr. Connell gave him a warm look. As Billy reached the front door he turned back around toward his parents.

"Dad?" Billy said.

"Yeah, Son?" Mr. Connell replied.

"You better take all the guns out of the house," Billy said.

Mrs. Connell lowered her head. Mr. Connell pushed his bowl of cereal away from him. He looked over at his wife, then up at Billy.

"I already have," he dejectedly replied.

The next day, Billy leaned against a fence post of the horse corral as he watched Joseph watch the sunset—a bright, orange glow that slowly descended over the distant mountain range. As the sun finally disappeared, it left behind a rainbow haze in the sky.

Joseph turned his wheelchair around and faced Billy.

"I have to go," he said to his big brother.

"Joey, you should be here, with your family," Billy replied.

"I can't just sit here and watch other people live," Joseph said.

"But...you've never so much as been across the Montana state line in any direction. I mean, India's far away. It's, it's...different over there," Billy said back.

"I know no one believes it, maybe not even the guy I'm going to see," Joseph said.

"I checked it out, Joey. I don't know what you can find over there. It will break Mom's heart if you leave," Billy said.

"It will break Mom's heart more if I stay," Joseph replied.

The sad meaning was not lost on Billy.

Joseph sighed.

"Will you take me?" he asked.

With a heavy heart, Billy nodded his head in agreement. He gently walked over to his baby brother's wheelchair and pushed him back toward the house.

Chapter 6

Three days later, Joseph sat in his wheelchair outside the Connell house as Billy drove his pickup truck up along side him. Very soon they would be flying nineteen hours on a plane to India. These two brothers, neither even old enough to legally consume alcohol, would be traveling halfway around the world in search of a fantastical elixir that a teenage boy needed to believe could be found.

Billy's wife, Elizabeth, holding their baby boy, James, stood next to Joseph. Mr. and Mrs. Connell walked out of the house to join them, with Mr. Connell carrying Joseph's lone, small suitcase. Billy stepped out of his truck, took the suitcase from his father, and placed it in the back of the pickup truck. Mrs. Connell opened the passenger door to the pickup truck as Mr. Connell reached down and scooped his maimed boy in his arms and placed him on the passenger seat.

Billy put Joseph's wheelchair in the flatbed of his pickup truck. Mr. Connell stared at Joseph for a moment without speaking, then simply said, "I love you, Joey, and I always have."

He reached up and took the orange baseball cap off his head, placed it on Joseph's disheveled hair, and hugged him.

"Take this. I hear it's damn hot over there. Hotter even then Montana," Mr. Connell said to Joseph, then stepped back to let Mrs. Connell say her goodbye.

She gave her baby boy a tight hug as she pressed her cheek against his. With affection and unconditional support whispered, "I knew you would leave us someday. Come back when you're ready. We'll always be here for you."

Joseph sat in the window seat of the plane with Billy next to him. It had been a long flight and the brothers were tired. They were flying into unchartered territory and had been silent most of the trip. Joseph looked out the window at the gravel-covered mountains thousands of feet below. The reflection of the sun's rays made the mountains appear a pale gold, broken up only by shadows cast from higher ridges.

The flight attendant spoke over the loud speaker to the passengers.

"Ladies and gentlemen, we will be landing in New Delhi, the capital of India, in about thirty minutes. The captain has asked that you please fasten your seatbelts for the remainder of the trip. On behalf of the entire crew, we would like to say thank you for flying India Express and we hope you enjoy your stay in our country," she said.

An hour later, Billy pushed Joseph through the airport as they made their way toward the exit to catch a taxi cab. The inside of the New Delhi airport was completely modern, right down to the vending machines with cans of soda for sale that they would find at their local supermarket back home.

The most striking difference initially to both brothers was the in clothing. While some Indians were dressed in familiar western clothes of pants and dress shirts, many others were attired in traditional Indian clothing. Most of the women were dressed in bright, vibrantly colored saris—a silk or cotton one-piece garment that covered the body from the shoulders right down to the ankles. Other women were dressed, also in a bright assortment of colors, in two-piece cotton outfits—cloth pants with a long shirt that flowed down to the knees. Some of the men were dressed in similar two-piece outfits of white, while some wore turbans.

The men who wore turbans were members of the Sikh religion, founded in India back in the fifteenth century. Its followers believed in obtaining peace and salvation through positive actions and pursuing their reunion with God.

India was also the birthplace of Buddhism. Its founder, the Buddha, born a Hindu prince in 573 B.C. in northern India, determined that the cause of suffering was an out of balance attachment to desire.

The majority of Indians—eighty-five percent— were Hindus. Hinduism was the world's oldest religion, with its holy scriptures—The Vedas—dating back five thousand years. It was a religion that encompassed yoga, ahimsa (non-violence), reincarnation, karma, mystical insights, epic mythologies, and one true God who could take millions of different forms and be known by millions of different names.

Yet, unlike the other major religions of the world, the origin of Hinduism could not be traced to one original founding person. It was a highly devotional religion, with daily offerings to the God (or Gods) of one's preference.

These two young brothers had just entered a most enigmatic country, where Nirvana was believed to exist, but only for those who could understand how the senses misled and the eyes were incapable of true sight.

Joseph was busy drinking in his new surroundings when Billy pushed his wheelchair over to a nearby currency exchange counter to exchange their American dollars for the local currency of Indian rupees. Since each U.S. dollar was worth forty-five rupees, Billy was handed many more bills back than he had handed over, including several coins.

He handed a random silver coin to Joseph.

"Here, Joey, hold onto this coin. Maybe it will bring you good luck," Billy said.

Joseph took the coin from Billy and looked at the heads side first. He felt it was quite ornate for a coin. It had a big number five in the middle. Above the five was some writing in Hindi he didn't understand. Under the number five was the word rupees, all in capital letters. Below that was the year it was printed, 1999.

On either side of the large number five was some type of floral arrangement that he assumed was of a native flower. Around the edge of the coin was an embroidery pattern. He was rather impressed with such a detailed coin design. It made him wonder what was on the tails side.

He flipped it over by gently flicking it with his thumb, sending it over the back of his left index finger. He moved his hand closer to his face to get a good look.

Billy stood behind him counting and recounting the large stack of rupee bills he had been handed.

When Joseph saw what was on the tales side of the five rupee coin, a paralyzing chill came over him and he nearly stopped breathing.

It was the statue of the four lions, perched atop the pillar, who all came to life in his nightmare and violently attacked him.

Billy had finished counting the money when he noticed Joseph staring at the coin and not moving.

"What's up, little brother?" he asked.

Joseph could barely speak in a low whisper.

"Lions," he said in a daze.

"What?" Billy asked, unable to hear him.

"Lions," Joseph repeated, still in a daze.

"Oh, yeah, lions. Well, we put an eagle on our quarter. I'm sure some other countries use a bear or a horse, well maybe not a bear exactly. Anyway, I read about that. Those lions are the emblem of India. It's been India's official emblem since 1950," Billy said.

The more Joseph learned, the more shaken he became.

"The emblem of India?" he asked, still in a fog.

"Yeah, something about an ancient emperor, I think. Pretty cool," Billy continued.

Joseph clasped at the coin as Billy put the money away in his pocket and proceeded to push Joseph to the airport exit.

As they made their way outside to the taxi area, they were immediately struck by the heat outside. Having grown up in Montana they were not unaccustomed to high temperatures, but this this heat was thick and heavy in a way they had never experienced.

There were dozens of taxi cab drivers waiting outside, but Billy made eye contact with one in particular whose warm smile was inescapable. The man walked directly up to them.

"Come. I will take you where you desire," he said while taking Joseph's suitcase as if he had known them for years and was here at the airport specifically to pick them up for the hundredth time. The taxi cab driver was not only exceedingly friendly in tone, but also in body language, as was the custom in India.

He offered them the sincerity of friendship as if he had known them for years. The fact that he had never met them before was no impediment to this. As he spoke, he tilted his head to the side as he gently gestured with his hand in a guiding motion. His body language and hand gestures, like that of all his countrymen, were soft, fluid, and non-aggressive, as if to say, "as you wish," without the need for actual words.

Billy felt more than a bit overwhelmed and saw no reason to look a gift horse in the mouth. He pushed Joseph's wheelchair to the rear passenger door and opened it to let Joseph lift himself the back seat.

While the Connell pickup trucks were too high for Joseph to be able to lift himself into using his one good limb, this taxi cab in India was the perfect height for him to be able to do so.

Billy sat in the back seat next to Joseph and handed the taxi cab driver the address on a piece of paper. The taxi cab driver looked it over and smiled.

"My friend, this address is very far away. You will get there much faster by train. I will drive you to the train station," he said.

"Thank you," Billy responded.

PAUL H. MAGID

Joseph said nothing, still unable to as yet fully recover from the shock of the lions that attacked him
being on the back of the first coin he came across.

As the taxi cab carrying the two brothers left the
airport and merged onto local highway roads, it was as
if they had been transported magically into their very
own Wizard Of Oz world. The air was pungent. Not
polluted, but thick with life.

The roadways were an endless sea of humanity and
animal life that all moved like raging rapids coursing
in every direction at once.

Cars, large commercial trucks carrying thousands
of sun-baked brick, and endless motorcycles shared
the roads with elephants, goats, camels, bicycle taxi
rickshaws (a three-wheeled bicycle with a carriage for
carrying passengers), motor scooters, pedestrians, and
water buffalo pulling carts loaded with vegetables.
Each participant in this endless orchestra of movement clamored for the right of way on the congested
asphalt.

All of these disparate roadway travelers moved
within feet or even inches of each other, yet no one,
except these two boys from Montana, seemed the least
bit perturbed by this arrangement.

What seemed like thousands of horns shrieked
relentlessly, not in anger, but as a necessary means
of communication to avert a million accidents that
seemed about to happen any second. The eardrums
of Billy and Joseph were accustomed to the soothing
sounds of nature in Montana, not the cacophony of

82

swooping vehicles and animals that shared these road-ways.

Billy and Joseph stared in shock as they passed a family of five all riding on one motorcycle. The father drove the motorcycle, while his three-year-old daughter sat on the gas tank between his legs, his five-year old son sat behind him, but in front of his mother, who held the youngest member of the family—a one-year-old baby.

Not one member of this daring family of five wore a helmet nor seemed to be the least bit concerned about dodging trucks, slow moving animals, or even the taxi cab the brothers were traveling in. Billy could see the tension in his little brother's face as he clutched at the handle above the window, to hold himself upright.

"We're not in Kansas anymore, Toto," Billy said, as he collected his wits about him and smiled at Joseph.

Billy's attempt to soothe Joseph worked.

"Well, if I'm Toto, I guess that makes you the girl, Dorothy," Joseph playfully answered back.

As traffic slowed to a crawl, the brothers couldn't help but notice that a man riding an elephant sat atop the multi-ton creature while talking on his cell phone—which perfectly represented India's parallel existence of the past interwoven with the present, the ancient and the modern together forming the fabric of India.

The roadway leading to the train station was filled with potholes, causing the taxi cab carrying the two brothers to bounce up and down over and over again.

The taxi cab driver looked in his rear view mirror to see how the brothers were doing.

"This roadway is called 'digestion alley,'" he said to them, while driving with his right hand and gesturing in a circular motion in front of his stomach with his left hand.

"Very good for the internal organs to process the food stuff. We have here in India many modern and most perfectly smooth roads, but this road is my most favorite for after a meal," he said.

He smiled at Billy and Joseph and they smiled back at him. The taxi cab finally pulled into the train station a few minutes later. The taxi cab driver turned around to face the brothers.

"Sir, may I again please see the address to which you are traveling?" he asked.

Billy gladly handed him the piece of paper showing the address.

"Yes, yes," said the taxi cab driver, "take this train to Haridwar and from there you can hire another local taxi as far as he will take you into the Himalayas. From there you can hire a farmer to take you by oxen."

"Oxen? Couldn't you just drive us. We'll pay you whatever you want," Billy said to this kind man.

"Sir, firstly, as I mentioned, you will get there much faster by train than by my taxi. Secondly, a car cannot navigate to this place you seek. There are no roads at the top of the earth. I cannot say for sure that there are even people there," he said while smiling at Billy.

"Okay. Thanks," Billy replied.

"Sir, may I ask you a question?" the taxi cab driver said to Billy.

"Sure," Billy replied.

"Well, sirs, India is the most beautiful country in the whole world. She has magnificent temples. She has the greatest expression of love ever witnessed, the brilliant Taj Mahal built by Shah Janan. She produces the world's finest silk, engineers, and has her own Silicon Valley. She is so modern that we not only have the Internet, but we have finally achieved insomnia," he said.

Billy and Joseph smiled at him.

The taxi cab driver was actually being modest in extolling his country's impressive achievements. India was the world's oldest civilization still in existence, whose roots could be traced back five thousand years. India's culture was already in her third millennium of existence when the upstart military societies of ancient Rome and Greece came to world power in the waning centuries of the ancient era.

India's spices were so desired by lands across the world that at the height of the Roman Empire, black pepper from southern India was literally worth its weight in gold as a means of monetary trading.

Despite defeating every army who stood before the soldiers of Rome, more than one Roman emperor feared the empire faced economic ruin because of its insatiable need for Indian spices, while having little that India desired in return.

It was India who gave to the world the invention of six-sided dice for means of game playing. It was India who was responsible ultimately for the creation of the modern computer age, for computers the world over run on a binary code of alternating ones and zeroes. Had a man from India not invented the concept of zero many centuries ago, the computer based world of today would not exist as it does.

Modern scientific technology has been able, through isotope carbon dating, to correctly estimate the current age of the known universe. Western science was a late comer to the party of determining the age of the universe, since ancient seers from India correctly determined that age thousands of years ago, simply by sitting still in meditation to learn all that needed to be known.

Perhaps the pleasant taxi cab driver assisting these brothers on their journey did not know all of these great achievements of India, or perhaps he simply did not want to brag too much. He continued his good-natured query of the brothers.

"Why then do you wish to go to this place up in the heavens where time does not exist?" he asked.

Billy looked over at Joseph, who had suddenly stopped smiling.

"Because I need to find someone," Joseph finally replied for Billy.

"Well then," said the taxi driver, "you will be okay, my friend. Karma has brought you both here for a reason and I am sure that it is a good one. Do not be afraid."

The taxi cab driver leaned over the seat and warmly looked Joseph directly in the eyes.

"You, my friend," he said to Joseph, "from the looks of things, Karma has for you very great plans."

"Thank you," Joseph softly replied with genuine appreciation.

After several hours on the train heading north into the Himalayas, Joseph and Billy looked out the window of the train and took in the fertile scenery of the Punjabi plains—India's breadbasket of wheat fields that stretched for hundreds of miles.

As they looked out the window, they sat alone on a bench seat meant to hold three people. Across from them sat four men shoulder to shoulder. Another man walked into their train car looking for a seat. He made no attempt to sit next to the brothers, but rather sat down on the crowded bench seat across from them. The four men already sitting on the bench all moved closer together so that he could sit down.

Joseph and Billy looked at each other, then at the men sitting across from them.

"Please, come sit here," Billy said to the Indian man who had just sat down across from them.

"No, sir, I cannot. That is quite all right," replied the man.

"But we have room," replied Billy.

"We have right here plenty of room, sir. You are a guest in my country. You take all the room you wish. We will no doubt fit another man at the next stop," replied the man.

Billy looked at Joseph, then back at the man.

"Thank you," he said to the man.

By midnight, Billy and Joseph were fast asleep on the train that was traveling overnight to their destination. They had laid down on the same bench seat they had been sitting on. Joseph slept on the inside of the bench, between the wall and his older brother.

At seven o'clock in the morning the train's ticket official woke the brothers up with a gentle shake.

"Sirs, we are at your destination in Haridwar," he said.

Billy got up first and got Joseph's wheelchair down from the overhead storage shelf. Joseph raised himself to a seated position and tried to shake off the cobwebs of the night's sleep as Billy also retrieved Joseph's suitcase.

The brothers found a local taxi and within a few minutes had begun the next leg of their journey. Haridwar was one of India's holiest cities, located along the Ganges River. Indians for century upon century have believed that simply bathing in this sacred river could wash away a person's sins. The city was located at the base of the Himalayan mountain range.

The Himalayas were the world's youngest mountain range, having formed one hundred and fifty million years ago when the diamond shaped Indian subcontinent broke away from the continent of Africa and slammed into the Asian continent. The force of the collision caused the land mass beneath the ocean to rise up from deep within the earth to form the highest mountain ranges on earth, the Himalayas.

Hindus of India believed that these majestic, heavenly mountain ranges were the home of their many Gods. They were not only the youngest and tallest mountain ranges in the world, but they were still growing at two millimeters per year, perhaps in order to provide future homes for future Gods.

As Billy and Joseph sat in the back seat of their taxi cab that climbed thousands of feet higher into the air, it was easy to see why Hindus believed these mountain peaks were the places that their Gods slept. For hours, the two brothers drank in every new mountain peak, each one distinctive from the one that preceded it.

Some had steep rock faces with little or no vegetation. Some were snowcapped, while an adjoining mountain top might be adorned in a thick covering of pine trees.

As the Ganges River flowed beneath the pine trees, the majestic landscape was the perfect place for ancient seers to pursue their work of discovering the secrets of the universe. Both Billy and Joseph were struck by not only how beautiful these ever climbing mountain ranges were, but how familiar they felt, as if they could have been mountain peaks in their home state of Montana. It was Joseph who first broke their silence.

"I didn't expect to see pine trees here. I wonder if they're ponderosa pine?" he said.

"I don't know," Billy replied. "I guess trees are trees."

Joseph burst out laughing, only too happy to release the tension.

"That's your great insight? Trees are trees?" he asked.

Billy smiled at him and just shrugged his shoulders as if to say, 'Yeah, that's all I got.'

As they continued their drive up the narrow Himalayan mountain road, they saw cattle being shepherded by entire families in some places, yet simply by teenage boys and girls along other stretches of road. The trip continued for several more hours in silence.

The drive through the Himalayas was an endless series of hairpin turns every fifty yards or less. It was a challenge for a fully, physically able person like Billy to keep his balance as the taxi cab threw him from side to side as it entered each turn. Joseph did not have the advantage of using his legs and feet to use as counter balance pressure on the floor of the taxi cab to help hold him upright.

All he had was his one good limb that had to keep his maimed body from being tossed to and fro at each sharp turn.

Billy couldn't help but notice the tensed forearm muscles of his little brother's arm straining to do the work needed for his entire body, as he clutched unceasingly at the door handle above the window. It was grueling, but Joseph would never complain. He noticed Billy staring at his arm.

"I'm okay," he said to Billy.

The truth was that Joseph's arm was killing him from the fatigue, but he held onto that handle above the door window as if his life depended upon it, because for him it did. A few minutes later, the taxi cab driver stopped when the road ended. He turned around to his passengers.

"I cannot take you any further, but wait here. I will find a farmer to take you in his oxen pulled cart," he said to Billy.

"Thank you," Billy replied.

Joseph gratefully let go of the handle over window and let his dead tired arm drop to his lap. As Billy stepped out of the taxi cab to pay the driver, Joseph let his head collapse back onto the top of the seat. He was drained and wanted to cry, but would neither quit nor let it show.

Still hours later, the brothers found themselves making their way in the back of this oxen pulled cart. Joseph sat in his wheelchair, which for him was a welcome relief, and Billy sat on the wooden floor of the cart, using his body as a way of keeping Joseph's wheelchair from moving.

The heat was sweltering. There were no longer any roads or even discernible paths. The entire small valley within this mountain peak range was compartmentalized into mini farms, with fields of crops in green, yellow, and red, so deep and bright they were visually intoxicating.

The brothers saw men and boys working the fields as women and girls carried the cut crops in large wicker baskets on their heads. Even here, high up in the mountains, in families that led subsistence lives, the women and girls were dressed in brightly colored saris.

Finally the farmer stopped his cart and pointed off into the distance.

"You will from here have to walk," he said.

Billy looked up at Joseph, who just nodded his head okay. Billy stood up and put Joseph's suitcase on the ground. He then lifted Joseph out of his wheelchair and placed him on the wooden seat next to the kind farmer. Next he lifted Joseph's wheelchair from the back of the cart and placed it on the ground next to Joseph, who lifted himself back into his wheelchair. While Billy paid the farmer, Joseph put his small suitcase on his lap.

As the farmer drove his oxen-pulled cart back into the direction from which they had come, Billy began pushing Joseph's wheelchair along the flat, bare, naked earth. Neither brother spoke for the hour it took before they both saw off in the distance a small one story white, stone house, situated at the bottom of a rock mountain.

As the tired brothers made their way closer to the lone house, they could see a small Indian man outside working in the garden. He looked up and saw them as well. He stopped gardening and walked into his house, where he filled a cloth container with water he poured from a copper pitcher. He then picked up a blue hat with a wide brim that would fully cover a man's face and neck, and walked just outside his front door.

As Billy finished pushing Joseph to the man's front door, Joseph realized that the man he had been sent to see was Lahiri, the sage who inexplicably visited him in the locker room the night he was maimed.

Joseph was momentarily disoriented, partly from this realization, partly from the grueling journey, and partly just from the heat. As he took a moment to gather himself together, Lahiri took the opportunity to use his extra sensory vision—which had little if anything to do with the retina of the eyeball passing electrical charges up to the brain—and peered directly into Joseph's body.

It was a special vision acquired from untold years of meditating—sitting still and doing nothing so that everything became visible—until the genuine nature of the universe manifested itself to him from within. He could see Joseph's aura—the flowing field of energy that surrounded his physical body.

Throughout recorded time, from the earliest of ancient eras through to the modern day, those possessed with the gift of sight—whether clairvoyant, spiritual seer, shaman, religious saint, or medical intuitive—speak with a universal voice on the nature of the human aura.

It is described as an "ethereal body" of energy, composed of a substance finer than the physical body. It is an alchemistic and energetic projection of the person, and the first grain of sand on the as yet mostly undiscovered beach of the grand universe that exists within and without, but is hidden to those who see with the eyes, feel with the hands, and hear with the ears.

To advanced adepts such as Lahiri, the physical world, witnessed at a deeper level of reality, was nothing more than layers of vibrating energy. He could see that Joseph was encased in a blue light—a good sign— but that it was a checkered, flickering, weak pulse of light, and broken up in several places.

He took all the time he needed, for time was a relative perception, and for Billy and Joseph, not even a full second had yet passed as Lahiri continued to peer into Joseph's energy field.

As he looked deeper, he could see where Joseph's neck had been gruesomely broken and where the nerves along his cervical spine had been severed and were no longer capable of sending electrical charges down his spine to enable his legs and right arm to move.

Lahiri let his gaze drift into Joseph's heart, where he could see the lion that had Joseph trapped on the ground and the other three that formed a menacing circle around him. Using his special abilities, Lahiri lifted the vision from Joseph's heart into a life-sized three-dimensional hologram in front of him, so that

Billy and Joseph were unknowingly smack in the middle of the unfolding battle.

After a few seconds, Lahiri returned the vision to Joseph's heart, and then broke the momentary, for the brothers, silence.

"I see the ice did not work," he said to Joseph, and smiled at him.

Lahiri's smile succeeded in getting Joseph to relax and speak up. Billy simply stood quietly behind his little brother's wheelchair.

"Can you help me?" Joseph asked Lahiri.

"For what are you searching?" Lahiri replied.

"To walk again," Joseph answered.

"Why?" Lahiri asked him.

"So..." Joseph gulped before contining, "So, I can live my life."

"Were you living it before?" Lahiri asked.

Joseph became flustered and didn't know what to say.

"Please may I see your hand?" Lahiri asked.

Joseph extended his left hand to Lahiri and closed his eyes, desperately awaiting his first mystical experience. Lahiri removed Joseph's watch from his wrist and handed it to Billy.

"He will not be having a need for this," Lahiri said to Billy.

Lahiri continued to hold Joseph's hand in his hands to soothe him.

"Would you like to come in?" Lahiri asked Billy.

Billy looked down at his baby brother, then back up at Lahiri.

"No, but thank you. I've got to get going," Billy said to Lahiri.

Lahiri let go of Joseph's hand so that he could hand Billy the blue hat and water jug he had been holding under his arm.

"Please take these," Lahiri said to him.

Billy nodded his head in gratitude. Lahiri picked up Joseph's suitcase from his lap.

"I will wait for you inside," he said to Joseph.

As Lahiri walked inside the front door of his small home, Joseph turned his wheelchair around to look at his big brother.

"I could stay awhile, I mean, if you'd like," Billy said to Joseph.

"I've got to get started," Joseph replied.

"Yeah," Billy said. "The sooner you start, the sooner you get back home."

"Right," Joseph answered.

Billy looked around at the strange new land his brother was choosing to call home. He wanted to ask his little brother what he could possibly find there that was worth being away from the family that loved him so dearly, but he did not. Instead, he bent down and hugged his little brother. He wished they had hugged more often. He finally let go of Joseph and began his long walk back toward civilization.

Joseph turned his wheelchair around and made his way through Lahiri's front door. The threshold to the door wasn't completely flush with the ground, though Joseph had no problem getting his wheelchair through the door. He didn't notice the small pile of twigs that had been freshly placed there just an hour ago to make sure he would have no problem getting into the house.

Joseph looked around the inside of his sparsely furnished new home. The center room had a small, modest wooden table with only one chair. To his left was the kitchen area with just a few shelves and no modern conveniences or even running water for the sink.

Lahiri emerged from the back room on the left side of the house.

"This is your room," he said to Joseph.

Joseph wheeled himself into the doorway of his new room, which actually had no door but rather a purple drapery cloth for privacy. Inside his room, he could see a small wooden desk, but no chair.

Also inside the room was a simple bed, a wooden night stand, and an oil lamp. The window was also covered by a thin, white cloth.

The bed had a unique bar running the length of the top of the bed, held in place by two vertical posts, so Joseph wouldn't have any trouble lifting himself into bed with his one good limb. He finished looking around his room, then wheeled himself back into the center room where Lahiri waited for him.

Lahiri pointed to the second room, next to Joseph's.

"That is my room next to yours. Are you hungry?" Lahiri asked.

"Thirsty," Joseph replied.

Lahiri walked to the kitchen area and poured water into a wooden cup, then walked back to Joseph and handed it to him. Joseph eagerly gulped the water down.

"Thank you," he said.

"You are welcome, Joseph," Lahiri replied.

"How does meditation work?" Joseph asked.

"It frees the soul from its bondage," Lahiri replied.

"I read that you were once buried for six days and lived off of one breath," Joseph said.

"I have big lungs," Lahiri replied.

"They say you can outrun a horse without breaking a sweat," Joseph inquired.

"Downhill perhaps. I am a great tumbler," Lahiri said while smiling.

"Does it, um, take long to learn mind over matter?" Joseph asked.

"Do you have somewhere to go?" Lahiri asked back.

"Well, no," Joseph sheepishly replied.

"You should. It is very hot in India," Lahiri joked.

Joseph relaxed and smiled gratefully.

"That was a tough fight I saw," Lahiri said.

"Yeah, it was just my time, I guess," Joseph replied.

"Your brother could have stayed," Lahiri said.

"He's got a wife and baby waiting for him back home," Joseph said.

"Family is important. Family is the most important thing there is in life," Lahiri said.

"Yeah," Joseph replied.

"What makes you think I can teach you to walk?" Lahiri asked.

"Because I need you," Joseph answered with pure, defenseless vulnerability.

Lahiri smiled earnestly.

"You should rest now. You have much work ahead of you," Lahiri said.

"I am tired," Joseph replied.

Joseph wheeled himself into his room and over to his new bed. Outside his bedroom window, the sun had just begun to set. He positioned himself by the side of his bed, reached up with his left arm, grabbed the perfectly placed bar, and pulled himself onto the thin mattress. Within moments his exhausted body drifted off into a deep sleep.

Lahiri walked into Joseph's room and over to his bed. He stood over Joseph and gently caressed his forehead for the second time.

"Welcome home, Joseph," Lahiri whispered.

Chapter 7

Joseph was awakened the following morning by the rising sun. He cleared the cobwebs and lifted himself into his wheelchair, using the bar above his bed. As he made his way to the purple cloth draped in his doorway, he suddenly stopped and turned his wheelchair around to look back at his bed.

His gaze started at the vertical bar near his pillow, worked its way across the top of the bed horizontally, and finally he looked at the second vertical bar at the end of his bed. He stared at it for another moment, then wheeled himself out into the main room of the house where Lahiri sat at the table with breakfast ready—a brown lentil dish, whole wheat circles of thin bread called *rotis*, and a bowl of home-made yogurt. Also on the table was a pitcher of water.

"Good morning, Joseph. Please, eat, eat," Lahiri said.

Joseph was famished and didn't have to be told twice. He watched Lahiri scoop the lentils onto a *roti* and use it as a sort of edible plate. Lahiri seemed to be enjoying the food, so Joseph couldn't wait to dig in.

He copied Lahiri's action, but as soon as he bit into the food, his mouth was on fire from the hot spices. He instantly reached past the pitcher of water for the bowl of yogurt and gulped down the entire bowl.

"God damn, that's hot," Joseph protested.

"How did you know the yogurt would cool your mouth much faster than the water?" Lahiri asked.

"I don't know," Joseph replied.

"Interesting," Lahiri said.

Joseph noticed a snake crawling on the wooden floor near their feet under the table. He reached down with his left hand and grabbed it, as he had done countless times back on his family's ranch in Montana, by the back of its head so it couldn't use its fangs to inflict a painful bite, or so Joseph thought.

"Jesus Christ, there's a snake in here," Joseph howled.

"Please, Joseph, do not be so rude," Lahiri replied.

Lahiri walked over to Joseph and took the snake from him. He then turned the head of the snake toward himself.

"Do not be angry with Joseph, my friend. He is not housebroken yet," Lahiri said to the snake.

"Me?!" Joseph exclaimed. "I save you from getting bitten by a snake, possibly a poisonous one, and I'm the one who's not housebroken?"

"Bitten? By my friend? Do not be so ridiculous. Never. He came looking for food, which in this case happens to be unwanted rodent intruders who will try to eat our crops before we have a chance to pick them," Lahiri said.

He gently placed the snake back on the floor where Joseph had found it and watched it slither away.

"Well," Joseph protested, "you could at least be impressed that I managed to catch it."

"I will be impressed when you catch it with your right hand," Lahiri said, while smiling.

Joseph smiled back at him.

With the breakfast excitement over, Lahiri walked over to his devotion table, which was between the front door and the kitchen area. On the table were necklace garlands of beautiful flowers, lying in front of a two-foot-high statue in a seated position. It had the body of a human, with four arms instead of two, and the head of an elephant.

Lahiri placed the garlands of flowers around the elephant-headed statue's neck. Joseph wheeled himself over to the devotion table and watched Lahiri place the flowers around the statue's neck.

"What are you doing?" he asked Lahiri.

"This is Lord Ganesha, the Remover Of Obstacles. I am performing a Puga. It is a daily offering of devotion," Lahiri said.

"It looks like an elephant head on a person's body. You're offering flowers to an elephant God?" Joseph asked.

"That is correct, Joseph. Hinduism has millions of Gods, all representations of the One True God. Each of the Gods has a purpose. I do this every day," Lahiri replied.

"The Remover Of Obstacles? You think giving flowers to an elephant-headed God is going to help remove obstacles?" Joseph inquired.

"It cannot hurt," Lahiri replied, while smiling at Joseph.

"Why does he have four arms?" Joseph asks.

"So he can remove obstacles twice as fast," Lahiri replied.

Lahiri finished placing the garlands of flowers around Ganesha's neck, then walked outside. Joseph followed him in his wheelchair, but as soon as he made his way outside, the hot Indian sun hit his badly sunburned skin from his travels the day before.

He frantically switched his wheelchair into reverse and made his way back to the safety of the inside of Lahiri's house.

"Holy crap, it's an oven out there," Joseph said to himself.

He looked down at the badly sunburned skin on his arms and felt the redness on his face. Lahiri walked back into the house holding long green stalks from a plant he had just picked. Inside the green stalks was fresh, jelly-like aloe vera. Lahiri pulled back the green outer stalks and rubbed the aloe vera onto Joseph's skin to soothe the sunburn.

"Wow, this stuff feels tingly and I can feel it cooling my skin down. But it smells like something that should have been thrown out six months ago," Joseph said.

"That is the plant's way of making sure you appreciate the sacrifice it has made for you," Lahiri replied.

"Thank you," Joseph said.

"Do not thank me. I am not the one cooling you off," Lahiri replied.

"So, you want me to thank a plant?" Joseph asked.

"Did the plant not relieve the pain of your sunburn?" Lahiri asked.

"Yeah, but it's just a plant," Joseph said.

"I see," Lahiri responded.

An hour later Lahiri was down on his hands and knees working in his garden beside his house. Joseph sat fidgeting in his wheelchair, with really nothing to do.

"Could we get started, please?" Joseph asked.

"We have. Today is Thursday. It is gardening day," Lahiri replied.

"I mean, could you start teaching me the mind over matter stuff?" Joseph asked.

"Oh, you mean, could I teach you the techniques of meditation so that you could transform your physical glandular hormonal secretions into a higher vibrational nectar of cosmic essence?" Lahiri said.

Joseph was oblivious to the sarcasm.

"Yes, yes, that is exactly what I want," he replied.

Lahiri stood up from his gardening duties.

"Well, then. Let us proceed," he said.

He pushed Joseph in his wheelchair several hundred yards away, to a flat open area of lush natural vegetation, and began giving Joseph the necessary instructions.

"Breathe, Joseph. Sit with your eyes closed. Take a deep breath, hold it for a few moments, and then take an even deeper breath. Hold it for as long as you comfortably can, then exhale. Feel the prana fill your body and connect you with the cosmos," Lahiri instructed him.

"What is prana?" Joseph asked.

"Prana is the life force of the universe that permeates everything you can see as well as everything you cannot. It is what makes the heat from the sun, the grass green, and a rock hard to the touch," Lahiri replied.

"That's it? Just sit here and breathe?" Joseph asked.

"Not exactly," Lahiri responded, "You must be very careful not to move."

"Because it will disturb my prana and prevent mind over matter?" Joseph asked.

"It is more like mind over death, really. If you move in this field, it is possible you may attract highly poisonous insects flying around this area and there is no antidote that I am aware of. Over many centuries countless would be devotees who could not sit still have met an untimely death right here in this exact spot," Lahiri said.

"But, I mean, nothing moves but my left arm anyway," Joseph replied.

"Then blame your left arm if you are stung and killed," Lahiri informed him.

Lahiri then turned and walked back toward his garden to finish his duties.

Over the next several days, Joseph spent every free waking moment following Lahiri's instructions so that he might experience the magical mind over matter phenomenon, yet nothing. It was late in the afternoon on his fifth day in India when he inhaled the largest breath he could force his lungs to accommodate, but still there was no change. He exhaled deeply, gave up, and began to cry.

Off in the distance, Lahiri watched him. There was in fact much more that his heart ached to share with Joseph, but it was not time...yet.

Several days later Joseph sat in his wheelchair with Lahiri next to him on a small embankment by the river. Night had just fallen and across the river Joseph could see a small temple and some kind of religious service going on.

Dozens of people had gathered for the event. The only light provided was from the partial moon out that night and fifty candles placed around a young teenage boy, as he sat directly in front of the local Hindu priest. To the boy's left was his mother and to his right was his father. The boy and his father, both dressed in white, were draped together under a white cloth. Joseph could see the priest looking at the boy's father as he imparted instructions.

"What's going on?" Joseph asked.

"This is Punal," Lahiri replied.

"What's Punal?" Joseph further inquired.

"It is the ceremony to celebrate the boy's passage from his life as a boy into his life as a man. He has completed the first phase of life and is now being prepared to enter his second stage," Lahiri replied.

"Why are they sitting like that?" Joseph asked.

"The father is passing on the wisdom every man must possess. But it is only to be spoken from father to son, and only this once. When the father is done, the priest will ask the boy many questions to determine whether he is ready to be recognized by their community as a man," Lahiri explained.

"What if the boy's answers are wrong?" Joseph asked.

"Oh, the father would not permit that to happen," Lahiri replied.

"How many stages of life are there?" Joseph asked.

"There are four. After adulthood comes seclusion to contemplate life and finally a man may return to society to be of service to others, if he wishes," Lahiri replied.

"How long do the stages last?" Joseph asked.

"Well, that depends on the person. It is not so very different from the West. It could be compared to your thirteenth birthday of confirmation, your twenty-first birthday of drunkenness, marriage, and finally your mid-life crisis by twenty-five," Lahiri said while smiling.

Joseph smiled back at him and Lahiri jumped at the opening he had worked so hard to create.

"Do you think about God much, Joseph?" Lahiri inquired.

Joseph's smile evaporated and a subtle scowl came across his face at the mention of that topic.

"No," was Joseph's curt reply.

"You do not wonder if He has a white beard and a thick wool robe to match?" Lahiri asked.

"No," was Joseph's curt reply again.

"Do you believe in God, Joseph?" Lahiri asked.

"Would it make a difference?!" Joseph snapped back.

He respectfully lowered his tone, partly in deference to Lahiri and partly so that he did not disturb the religious ceremony taking place across the river embankment.

"I just don't like Him very much," he said to Lahiri.

"And why have you judged God so harshly?" Lahiri replied.

Joseph tried to keep a lid on his anger, but it boiled over again.

"Because he's all powerful, right?! Mr. God-damned omnipotent, right?! So why does he make us suffer? For his fucking amusement?!" Joseph venomously answered.

Lahiri was unruffled by Joseph's outbursts.

"God does not punish, Joseph. God teaches," he calmly replied.

Joseph worked to calm himself back down.

"Well, he can keep his God-damned lessons. I've had all the teaching I can take. And what about… what about innocent people like me…like, like when someone hurts another person who didn't do anything wrong?" Joseph demanded.

"That is most certainly not God. One person hurting another is like a hand curling into a fist to smash the foot," Lahiri replied.

"It's still not fair. Why, why, why is it so easy for some and so hard for others?" Joseph pleaded.

"Life is never easy, Joseph. Not for anyone. We all have our battles to fight," Lahiri replied.

"But it's still not fair. God had no right to make me a cripple," Joseph said.

"The ancients believed that the universe did not exist for a man until he opened his eyes and created it," Lahiri answered.

"So I created a crippled?" a confused Joseph asked.

"Your soul is trying to tell you…it wants to go Home," Lahiri replied.

The next day Lahiri walked through a meadow not too far from the field where Joseph spent most of his waking hours meditating, without much progress. Many villagers used this meadow as a park area to have a leisurely lunch. Children of various ages played games, ranging from the universal game of tag (which required no equipment of course) to the game universally played throughout India—cricket.

Even more than soccer (which in India was called football, as in Europe), cricket was played by the rich and the poor. The rich might have had fancy sporting equipment, but the poor could enjoy the national obsession just as well with a ball, a handmade wooden stick, and enough open area to smack the ball with the wooden stick.

As Lahiri walked, he carried an American football, which was a sport unknown throughout India to the vast majority of people. He may very well have been the only Hindu in India carrying an American football. His plan was not to play, but to set in motion a play of his own.

He continued walking until he came across Vijay, a slender boy of eight years old wandering through the meadow by himself. His older sister, Madhu, aged eighteen, had given him a break from shepherding the family's cattle with her. She had brought them to a nearby field to graze on the native grass and told him to take a break since there wasn't anything that needed to be done until they finished grazing anyway. Vijay was about to walk over to some boys playing tag when Lahiri intercepted him.

He showed Vijay the football and explained to him that it was a very popular game in America. He showed him how to throw and catch the ball. Vijay, like any little boy his age, was naturally curious and eager to play with a new toy in the form of a football.

As Vijay tossed the ball gently in the air, Lahiri walked a short distance to three ten-year-old boys playing a game of tag. He greeted the boys warmly as he told them he had a job for them. He told them that it was really more of a joke. He pointed over to Vijay playing with the football and told them that in a few days he wanted them to take the football away from Vijay and wrestle him to the ground. None of the boys would agree to do it.

Lahiri took several rupee bills from his garment and offered to pay them one hundred rupees. They may have been young boys, but they knew how to strike a better deal. They demanded double, and for each of them.

Lahiri relented, but he said they got half the money upfront and half afterwards. He warned them though, if they hurt Vijay in any way, they didn't get the rest of their money. The boys told him they understood and the plan was set.

Later that night, Lahiri sat on the floor of his white, stone house while working on his simple wooden handloom. It had a spinning circle in the center which enabled him to spin the cotton into usable fabric.

Joseph sat in his wheelchair and watched.

"Have you always spun your own clothes?" Joseph asked.

"Not just me, Joseph, but millions and millions of Indians for over a thousand years have spun some of the world's finest fabrics. India has always been a country of riches, and not just her fabrics, but her spices, and raw materials. Such blessed wealth is what motivated many peoples, the Dutch, the French, the Portuguese, and many others to invade her over the centuries. But it was the British who conquered Mother India in 1757 and ruled her for nearly two centuries," Lahiri explained.

"I guess that explains why so many people in India speak English," Joseph replied.

"Yes, it does. The English brought a great many technological improvements that benefited India, including a modern system of law, thousands of miles of railroad tracks to transport materials and people, the postal service, the telegraph, and many, many more," Lahiri told him.

"Wow, then I guess India must be pretty grateful," Joseph replied.

"The English also brought starvation, famine, and suffering to millions of Indians by taxing them of their crops and earnings, and forcing them to buy imported English goods and fabrics. Some weavers, who made their living on a handloom just like this one, had their thumbs cut off by British soldiers so that Indians would need to pay for the fabrics imported from England," Lahiri said.

"Oh," replied Joseph.

"Yes, less than twenty-five thousand British soldiers managed to rule over millions of Indians, as incredible as it sounds," Lahiri said.

"I didn't know that. Did anyone in your family have their thumbs cut off?" Joseph asked.

Lahiri stopped spinning for a moment on his handloom and looked Joseph in the eyes.

"No, Joseph. No one in my family had their thumbs cut off," he said.

"Well, I'm glad to hear that," Joseph replied.

"The British soldiers who gave the orders to mutilate had good reasons, or so they believed. They did not consider themselves bad people. In fact, they considered themselves good people doing the right thing, who were simply acting for the 'greater good.' The problem is, we are all the 'greater good'," Lahiri said.

Joseph didn't know what to say. Lahiri decided to lighten the mood.

"India has always been a magical place. In her five-thousand-year history she has never attacked another country, though many others have sought out her shores," Lahiri said.

"I am amazed at how some people with so little can be so friendly," Joseph said.

"A person needs money or material possessions to be friendly?" Lahiri playfully jabbed at him.

"That's not what I meant," Joseph replied.

"The people of India, whether the richest of the rich, or the poorest of the poor, know that it is not what you have that matters, it is what you do. It is called Dharma," Lahiri said.

"What is Dharma?" Joseph asked.

"Dharma is what you are required to do if you are to advance spiritually. It is the work you must complete. It is your duty in life," Lahiri said.

Lahiri had Joseph's curiosity piqued.

"What is my Dharma?" Joseph asked.

"That is for you to discover. I cannot tell it to you," Lahiri replied.

"Oh," a disappointed Joseph said, but then asked, "What is your Dharma?"

"You are," Lahiri replied.

Joseph stared at Lahiri.

"That is why I saved your life in the woods the night you hit the deer," Lahiri replied.

Joseph was stunned at the news.

"That was you?" he whispered.

"It was," Lahiri replied.

"The police said someone used my cell phone to call for an ambulance," Joseph said.

"Yes, that was me," Lahiri replied.

"Why were you there?" Joseph asked.

"Because I knew what was going to happen," Lahiri replied.

Joseph was shocked and deeply hurt.

"But if you knew what was going to happen, you could have prevented me from being stuck in this wheelchair. Why didn't you do something before that deer broke my neck?" Joseph painfully asked.

"Would you have felt any better if the deer had fulfilled its Dharma the next day? Or the day after that? There are some things that cannot be stopped, once they have been set in motion, Joseph, no matter how much we wish they could. I tried to stop the deer that night from the locker room, but you turned me away," Lahiri replied.

Joseph was disoriented at the revelation and couldn't talk about this anymore. He wheeled himself away from Lahiri and toward his bedroom. When he reached the curtain hanging in his doorway he stopped pushing his wheelchair and looked back over at Lahiri.

"Thank you…for saving my life," he whispered, then wheeled himself into his bedroom before he could hear Lahiri's reply.

"I had to," Lahiri whispered, "I need you to save mine."

Chapter 8

In a dream, an able-bodied Joseph laughed and ran after two small Indian boys, aged five and two years old as they ran up a small grass covered hill. As he caught up to them, he tickled them both from behind. They squealed with laughter and mock protest.

"No tickling, Daddy," the older boy said.

The two-year-old boy, a pudgy little bundle of joy with a thick mop of black hair and still in his diapers, waddled out of sight over the hilltop. Joseph rubbed the older boy's belly as he tackled him and continued the tickling despite the prior protest. After another moment, Joseph stood to go after his younger son.

As he made his way over the hilltop, he saw his little boy on the ground in a pool of his own blood—his throat gruesomely slashed from ear to ear.

From behind him, Joseph suddenly heard his older boy cry out to him.

"Daddy!" the boy yelled.

A startled Joseph turned around, only to find his older son also on the ground, dead, in a pool of his own blood, his throat slashed the same as his little brother's.

An hour after waking from his nightmare, Joseph sat silently by the riverbed in his wheelchair and watched the rapids take the water downstream. The current was strong and would have no problem carrying him—how far he did not know, nor care.

With robotic precision, he reached with his left hand into the frame of his wheelchair and one by one took out the parts of the small 22-caliber gun he had disassembled and stored in the hollow metal frame. He laid each piece on his lap as he stared at the water, assembling the gun without the need to look at the individual pieces.

Joseph came to India brimming with hope born of desperate need, but also with doubt produced by a tired spirit—doubt in the form of a small handgun he knew could be easily hidden within the hollow recesses of his wheelchair.

Nearby, Lahiri watched.

Joseph turned his wheelchair so that his right side was close to the water's edge. He knew that even a small 22-caliber gun, shot at close range, would have enough force to send his toppled body and spirit into the river.

Joseph picked up the gun and pointed it at his left temple.

Still Lahiri did not move.

Joseph's hand trembled, but would not falter. He did not know what awaited him, if anything, on the other side, but it had to be better than what was constantly lying in wait for him on this side.

He slowly contracted the tiny muscles of his left index finger and pulled the trigger, desperate to stop the madness he could no longer endure.

The trip hammer pulled back until it had reached its loading tension, then fired forward. A shiver seized Joseph as he expected the end to blow a hole clean through his brain, but there was no blast.

He shivered again in an involuntary response and began to hyperventilate, wondering what had gone wrong. As he stared at the gun that fired, yet fired no bullet, Lahiri walked up to him quietly at first.

Joseph pulled his confused gaze away from the gun and up to Lahiri.

"It will not work, Joseph. I know. You cannot go around. You must go through," Lahiri said to him.

Lahiri then reached into his simple brown garment and pulled out one lone bullet—the bullet he had surreptitiously removed from Joseph's hidden wheelchair gun while he slept. He stared at the bullet a moment, then silently handed it to a bewildered Joseph.

Joseph was still staring at the bullet as Lahiri turned and walked away, back toward their house.

Hours later Lahiri sat alone at the table in his house and waited and waited and waited. Dinner sat in front of him, untouched. He wondered in painful rumination if his final act toward Joseph would, in fact, be his final act. Even hours of deep meditation could not replenish his depleted spirit.

He needed to see for himself what Joseph would choose to do. What would he say to Joseph's parents, who had entrusted their son to him, if he had made the wrong decision in giving Joseph back the bullet?

Finally, Joseph wheeled himself quietly into the house and up to the table to eat dinner. Joseph used the spoon to pour lentils onto a *roti*. Lahiri quietly followed his lead and began eating dinner, choosing first to add some vegetables to his plate.

After several moments, Joseph reached down into his lap, picked up the bullet, and placed it on the table in front of Lahiri, who said nothing as he reached for the bullet without saying a word. He simply took it and, with a lightened heart, placed it back into his garment.

Later that evening Lahiri sat on the floor again, spinning cotton on his wooden handloom. Joseph sat reading from a book he had found in Lahiri's house. He flipped the page he had just finished reading and found a coin in the book. He picked it up and stared at the tails side, looking at the date printed on it—1859.

"Where did you get this penny?" Joseph asked.

"It is a shilling," Lahiri replied.

"Oh," Joseph said.

"A man gave it to me once," Lahiri continued.

"He must have had it for a very long time," Joseph answered.

"Not really," Lahiri said, as he watched Joseph stare at the coin curiously.

"I wasn't sure your brother was going to leave you," Lahiri continued.

He watched Joseph put the coin back onto the page of the book he found it on, close the book, and put it down on the small wooden table next to his wheelchair.

"Billy never liked to leave me anywhere, not even at home. One summer he went to this sleep-away camp up in northern Montana and wanted me to go with him. I wanted to go too, problem was I was only eleven and Mom didn't want to let me go. It took him four days of convincing, but he finally got her to agree," Joseph said.

"Did you have a good time?" Lahiri asked.

Joseph was momentarily lost in pleasant thought.

"I met Hollie. First time she looked at me, I swear I didn't breathe for a whole minute," he said.

Lahiri sarcastically raised his eyebrows to acknowledge such a stupendous feat.

"Hey, for some of us that's still a long time to go without breathing. Anyway, I won spaz of the week because of her. If we were apart for too long, I sort of got disoriented and just wandered around until I found her. One night Billy made himself scarce and she came over to our cabin. I was so scared. Every time I tried to kiss her, I got light-headed," he said.

Lahiri smiled.

"What happened?" he asked.

"We kind of dated for the summer. But then... then...the visions came back, and I haven't seen her since," Joseph explained.

Lahiri's smile faded as a moment of silence dragged into two, then three. Joseph didn't want to think about that anymore.

"So, how did you, um, become a yogi?" he asked, redirecting the conversation.

"The correct term is sadhu, or sage, depending on whom you ask," Lahiri replied.

"My apologies. So, how did you become a sadhu, or sage, depending on whom you ask?" Joseph asked.

"Well, it is not exactly a profession," Lahiri replied.

"I know, but I mean, you know, was it 'predetermined by God,' or something?" Joseph asked.

"Not everything in life is predetermined, Joseph, not even by God. I once looked forward to sitting under the white cloth with my son as he would grow from a boy into man, someday. You have to be careful. What you whisper has to be loud enough for him to hear but not so loud that anyone else, including the priest can hear you, or he will ask your son impossibly hard questions," Lahiri said.

"Where is your family now?" Joseph asked.

"They were killed, in an accident," Lahiri replied.

"What kind of accident?" Joseph asked.

"An unfortunate one," Lahiri replied.

Joseph didn't know what to say.

"Why did you start karate, Joseph?" Lahiri asked.

"Because I thought it might help me escape...the visions," Joseph replied.

"You should not give up meditating," Lahiri said.

"But when I do, I just can't feel anything," Joseph answered.

"You will," Lahiri said back.

Several days later Lahiri arose especially early so that he could make sure he had a sufficient amount of brightly colored magenta powder, which he now had in his fists held down by his sides.

Joseph pushed his wheelchair out of his room to see what was for breakfast that day. When he passed through the curtain in his doorway, Lahiri threw the magenta powder all over him. Joseph was unprepared to be enveloped in a thick cloud of purple powder. He coughed several times, but the vegetable powder was harmless to his lungs.

"Happy Holi!" Lahiri exclaimed, with the exuberant glee of a small child.

Joseph finished coughing, then asked, "What the Hell is Happy Holi?"

"Well, it is not Happy Holi. It is just called Holi. I added the happy part. But to answer your question, Holi is the spring festival, celebrating the rebirth of life as the seasons change, and the death of Holika, an ogre goddess who devoured children," Lahiri said, still with an irrepressible smile of a child.

"Well, where's my powder?" Joseph asked suspiciously.

"You are wearing it. But there is more in town. If we leave now, we can still enjoy the parade," Lahiri said.

Joseph looked down at his purple covered body and wheelchair, nearly speechless.

"Holy cow. I swear this country finds something to celebrate every God-damned day," Joseph finally replied.

"And...this is a bad thing?" Lahiri playfully asked.

It took an hour for them to reach the festival in town, but it was well worth the trip. As they reached the outskirts of town they passed an assortment of street performers, snake charmers, monkey trainers, and *fakirs*—men who seemed to be performing feats of mind over matter, such as piercing their skin with needles but not bleeding.

As Lahiri pushed Joseph passed these performers, Joseph noticed one extremely impressive *fakir*, an old man who appeared to be levitating above the earth. He was draped in a white cloth and he held out in front of him a wooden cane, which was also draped in the white cloth.

It was obvious that he was levitating because there was clearly nothing underneath him that could be holding him up. The meditating *fakir* was in a complete state of quiet bliss as he hovered above the earth below.

Joseph was impressed.

"Wow. Maybe he could teach you some mind over matter tricks and then you would have something useful to teach me," Joseph playfully jabbed at Lahiri.

Lahiri looked over at the impressively levitating fellow.

"He is called a *fakir* and things are not always what they appear to be, Joseph," Lahiri replied.

"Maybe not," Joseph impetuously replied, "but so far that man has shown me more supernatural power than you have."

"Really?" Lahiri asked.

"Mmm..hmmm," Joseph replied.

Lahiri stopped pushing the purple powered covered Joseph in his purple powered covered wheelchair and walked over to the *fakir*, who of course ignored him because he was in deep cosmic supernatural meditation….though he did manage to jiggle his silver cup seeking a donation.

Lahiri looked back at Joseph, who just gave him a 'And what are you going to do?' look.

That was all the go ahead Lahiri needed. He gently shoved the man, as gently as a shove can be, anyway. The levitating *fakir* immediately fell over on his side to the dirt below, knocking the pretty white cloth off of him and his magical cane. As he rolled onto the ground, furious, the source of his alleged supernatural power became clear—the cane he was holding was attached to a horizontal piece of wood, which was then attached to the seat the *fakir* was comfortably sitting on, all of which was concealed by the serene white cloth.

It was an impressive feat of balance, to be able to hold himself up with just the cane for support, but it was not levitating and it was not supernatural.

Joseph burst out laughing as the furious charlatan yelled at Lahiri in his native language. He swung his hands wildly as he collected his wooden contraption and now not so white cloth and headed for another part of town to set up shop again where travelers may not have witnessed this unplanned revelation.

Lahiri walked back over to Joseph and returned to pushing his wheelchair closer to the parade going on in town.

"*Fakirs* have impressive balance, but I do not like *fakirs*. They give us sages a bad reputation as fakers," Lahiri said.

Joseph looked back at Lahiri smiling at him, then turned his attention back to the festival taking place ahead of him. As they joined the parade area, it became a large, moving cloud of brightly colored powder. Magenta was the dominant color of Holi, but also the air was filled with clouds of red, green, and yellow vegetable powders. Adults and children took part in the fun as brightly colored paper-mache costumes of local deities were paraded down the road.

Joseph saw a wooden table with piles of colored powder just waiting to be picked up and thrown, so he wheeled himself over to the table, grabbed what he could, and threw it on as many nearby people as he could. They, of course, did the same to him. The only thing more impressive than the clouds of flying powder was the laughter that everyone, from the smallest girl to the largest man, were enjoying as they celebrated the Holi spring festival.

Days later Joseph pushed himself in his wheelchair to the meadow that Lahiri had seen Vijay playing in when he gave him the American football. Normally Joseph would have spent this afternoon meditating, but Lahiri was adamant that he take the afternoon off and go enjoy the meadow, and Joseph wasn't about to refuse.

Along his way he saw the three ten-year-old boys on the ground that Lahiri had paid money to, and under them was Vijay. They seemed to be bullying him, but they weren't doing a very good job. At most, they were refusing to let him get back up.

"Come on, give us the ball," the biggest of the boys said to Vijay. Vijay was about as imposing as a leaf, but he wasn't giving up his, to him, one-of-a-kind ball.

Lahiri had given the three ten-year-old boys explicit instructions to not actually hurt Vijay, but even this attempt at bullying wasn't exactly an Oscar worthy performance.

Nevertheless, Joseph was upset by what he saw.

"Hey, get the hell off of him!" he yelled.

He wheeled himself over to the boys, and using his one good limb, threw them one at a time off of the dirt-covered Vijay, who still rather impressively clutched at his football.

The boys had been coached by Lahiri to not do anything to Joseph either, so they simply ran away without saying another word. Mostly, they were too interested in collecting the rest of their loot for what seemed like a pointless pretend moment. Lahiri was within sight of the incident, but behind several trees so he could not be noticed. He would go find his second rate actors later and pay them the rest of the money he had promised them.

Vijay stood up and dusted himself off.

"Are you okay?" Joseph asked.

"I will be fine," Vijay replied.

"What's your name?" Joseph asked.

"Vijay," the little boy replied.

"My name is Joseph. Is VJ short for something, like Victor James?" Joseph asked.

"Vijay is not my initials. It is spelled V-I-J-A-Y, Vi-jay," the little boy said.

"Okay, Vijay. Why were those boys picking on you?" Joseph continued.

"I do not know. They have never done so before," Vijay replied.

"Well, if you want, I can teach you to fight so they can't pick on you anymore," Joseph offered.

"You?" Vijay asked incredulously. "You cannot even walk. What can you teach me?"

Joseph snorted in response.

"What can I teach you, huh?" he said.

"Yes, what can you teach me?" Vijay innocently repeated.

Joseph looked around until he saw just the right sized piece of broken concrete by the side of the road, then pointed at it.

"Tell you what, little man, go grab that piece of broken concrete over there and I'll show you," Joseph replied.

"I do not understand why I should be picking up a piece of broken concrete," Vijay said back.

"Just go pick it up and I'll show you," a slightly flummoxed Joseph said.

"Okay, but it makes no sense to me," Vijay said, as much to himself as to Joseph.

Vijay did as he was told and picked up the broken piece of concrete and walked it back to Joseph. He tried to hand it to Joseph.

"Here you go," Vijay said.

"No, you hold it," Joseph replied.

"Okay, but what am I supposed to do with it?" Vijay asked.

"Just hold it out in front of you," Joseph instructed him.

Vijay did as he was told.

"Now, hold it there and don't let it move," Joseph told him.

Joseph took the deepest breathe he could muster, curled his left hand into the tightest fist he could, and smashed his fist into that broken concrete with all the rage and anger and frustration and heart-ache he had ever felt.

The concrete broke into five pieces as it fell from Vijay's stunned, little hands. Vijay looked down at the now smaller pieces of broken concrete as if he had just seen the most impressive magic trick of his life.

Joseph was a bit startled himself by his own action. He clenched and unclenched his fist, just to make sure nothing was broken. Except for a fairly good-sized trickle of blood coming from his knuckles where just a moment ago there was skin, he was fine.

He smiled as he took a deep breath, then looked up at a very impressed little Indian boy.

"Can you teach me to do that?" Vijay asked.

"Well, no, I can't. But I could teach you to fight in case those boys bother you again," Joseph answered.

"No, that is okay. They have never done so before and I do not think they should be having any need to do it again," Vijay replied.

"Suit yourself," Joseph said.

Vijay picked up the football Lahiri had given him.

"Do you know how to throw that thing?" Joseph asked.

"Not really," Vijay replied.

"Well, here, give it to me. My brother showed me when I was your age. You want to line your fingers up on the laces and then pull your hand back by your ear, then let the ball roll off your hand as you come forward," Joseph instructed while demonstrating.

A pleased Lahiri looked on for several moments before smiling as he walked back toward his home.

The next day Joseph sat meditating in the meadow when he was unexpectedly approached by Madhu, Vijay's eighteen-year-old older sister. She was slender and beautiful, standing five-feet, four-inches tall, with long dark hair, big brown eyes, and a bright infectious smile. She wore a brightly colored turquoise sari—her favorite color.

She stood patiently beside his wheelchair for several minutes and watched him, waiting for him to notice her.

He finally opened his eyes and saw her.

"Hel...hello," he said, surprised and more than a bit entranced.

"Hello. My name is Madhu. You are Joseph, yes?" she asked.

"Yes, I'm Joseph," he said.

"Thank you for what you did for my brother Vijay yesterday. For coming to his aid and for playing with him. He gets lonely sometimes since our father died last year," she said.

"Um, you're...you're welcome," Joseph said.

Madhu turned and began walking away.

"Wait," Joseph called out.

"Yes?" Madhu said as she turned back toward him.

"Where are you going?" Joseph asked.

"I have to walk our cattle up the road to feed on the grass," Madhu replied.

"Can I come with you?" Joseph asked.

"Yes," Madhu replied, smiling at him.

Minutes later, Madhu held a long, bamboo walking stick, which she gently swung it in the direction of the ten cows that meandered along on the road. Joseph pushed himself in his wheelchair along side her.

"You are from where, Joseph?" she asked.

"Montana. It's in America," he said.

"I see," she replied.

Joseph nodded.

"Vijay tells me that you broke a piece of concrete with your fist?" she said.

"Yeah, I learned it doing karate," Joseph replied.

"What made you start karate?" Madhu asked, while encouraging a laggard cow to keep moving with the rest of the small herd.

"It was just something to do," Joseph lied.

"You have so much free time in America you have to look for things to do?" she asked.

"Oh, no. My dad kept us plenty busy," Joseph said, and then caught himself, "I'm sorry about that, about your dad and all."

"It is okay," Madhu replied.

"Don't you get any time for yourself?" Joseph asked.

"When I am older, there will be time," Madhu replied.

"Is everyone up here a farmer?" Joseph asked.

"What else could they do, so far from the world? Most men and boys work in the fields or raise cattle like we do. A woman works in the fields with their husband, if that's what they do. Girls clean the house, do laundry, and wait to find a husband, to start their own family. Since our father died, Vijay and I help my mother," Madhu said.

"What will happen when you get married? I mean, as far as work and stuff with your mother and Vijay. Will you still live with them?" Joseph asked.

"Normally, I would move out into my husband's house to live with his family, but I will probably never know," Madhu said.

"Why is that?" Joseph asked.

"Because up here a girl needs a dowry to give her husband's family to get married," she said.

"What's a dowry?" Joseph asked.

"It is a gift from the bride's family to the husband's family at the time of marriage," Madhu said.

"I've never heard of such a thing," Joseph replied.

"I am told in the cities a girl has only to give her love to get married. We cannot afford to give up one of our cows because we need them to sell milk, so I may never get married," Madhu said.

"I see," Joseph replied.

"Why did you come to India?" Madhu asked.

"To find Lahiri. Do you know him?" Joseph asked.

The cows had made their way to delicious grass growing out of the side of the mountain, so Madhu sat down on a rock to let them graze. Joseph pushed his wheelchair up next to her.

"No one really knows him. I just know that he came down from the higher mountains when I was a little girl. There is a legend that he is three hundred years old. My great-grandmother once told me that her great-grandmother knew him as a boy. Others say he was never a boy and that he just appeared on earth as an old man," she replied.

"Oh. So, I guess no one knows anything about his family?" Joseph asked.

"I did not know he had a family. Where are they?" Madhu asked.

"He said they died in an accident," Joseph replied.

"Is that how you met?" Madhu asked.

"No. We just kind of found each other and he is teaching me to walk again," Joseph said.

"How?" Madhu asked.

"With the power of mind over matter, but it's not going so well so far," he replied.

"I see. How did you become disabled?" she asked.

"I was on my way home from a karate tournament and a deer jumped out into the road and wouldn't move. It ran me into a tree and I broke my neck," Joseph replied.

"Maybe it was someone dear," Madhu said.

"What's that supposed to mean?" Joseph asked.

"Maybe it was someone from a past life," Madhu replied.

"Do you really believe in reincarnation?" Joseph asked.

"There are over a billion people in India and most all of them believe in reincarnation," Madhu said.

"But, why?" he asked.

"Because it only makes sense. God is not cruel. He is trying to teach us what we need to learn, and giving us many opportunities to learn it," she said.

"But that doesn't make any sense. Every year there are more and more people in the world, so how could everyone be reincarnated?" Joseph asked.

"Firstly, Joseph, there is too much to learn in just one lifetime. Secondly, do you really think this little planet is the only place life exists in the universe?" she asked.

"So some of us were former aliens?" he replied.

"I do not know exactly. I only know what I believe…what makes you think Lahiri can teach you to walk again?" she asked.

"Because sages can do mind over matter, and when he teaches me I'll use it to walk with the power of the mind," Joseph answered.

"Do you know what the name Lahiri means?" she asked.

"No, I don't," he answered.

"It means, 'drunken one'," Madhu told him.

Weeks later, Lahiri stood outside his front door as he yelled back inside and beckoned for Joseph to join him.

"Hurry, Joseph! Hurry. You are going to make us late," Lahiri called.

Joseph wheeled himself outside.

"What's the big hurry?" he asked.

Lahiri pointed to the sky, which was heavy and full of dark clouds weighed down with water.

"See those clouds?" Lahiri asked.

"How could I miss them?" Joseph replied.

"Monsoon season is upon us. We must get into town before the rains begin so that we may contribute and pay homage for nourishing our crops," Lahiri said.

Two hours later and fifty yards from the outskirts of town, where the festival was in full swing, the skies opened up in a way that Joseph had never witnessed. Growing up in the Montana foothill mountains, he was not unaccustomed to heavy rains, but still he had never witnessed anything like this before.

India's lush greenery and foliage could be traced back to the unique weather pattern of the monsoon rains. They started at the southern tip of the Indian subcontinent in late May and worked their way thousands of miles north to the Himalayan mountain range by September. For most of India the three or four months of sometimes constant rain was all the rainfall they would receive all year, so it was very important for crops and the people whose lives depended directly on them.

The raindrops falling on Joseph were large enough to cause small animals to run for cover. Dozens of villagers were adorned in special ceremonial outfits, with bright colors and intricate, floral design patterns, garland after garland of flowers, and hand-crafted necklaces. Many had complicated tattoos on their hands and arms of henna—a vegetable dye. Others danced in elaborate routines, as was the custom at festivals, an expression of the appreciation for life itself.

Even those not dancing were nevertheless happily jostled from side to side, soaked to the bone, and completely happy. Joseph searched the crowd for Madhu. He found her across the street, dancing with several of her friends.

It took him a while and several attempts to make his way over to her in his wheelchair, but he did finally get close to her.

"Will I see you tonight?" he asked.

Madhu smiled and nodded her head yes.

By midnight the rains had tired of their onslaught and were resting until the morning. The moon was barely one quarter full, but still provided ample light for Joseph and Madhu. She sat on a rock next to his wheelchair as she played on a small flute. Her melody was beautiful in a soothing way—she was quite talented. When she finished her musical poetry, she placed the instrument down next to her on the rock.

"Providing entertainment to a husband's family is just one of the many important duties a wife must perform," she said to Joseph while smiling at him.

"You're worth it, just for the music," he said, while smiling right back at her.

"Tell me about your family, Joseph," she said.

"My dad owns a bottling plant back in Montana. My brother Billy runs it with him," he said.

"But you did not want to do that?" Madhu asked.

"What makes you say that?" Joseph asked, impressed by her intuitive abilities.

"If you did, you would not be here," she said back.

"Oh, right. No, I mean, the ranch is beautiful. Dad raises horses and stuff," he said.

"Why are you not married?" Madhu asked.

"Wow, you ask a lot of questions, but I like that, from you," he said back.

"What will happen when you get married?" he asked, even though she had already told him when they first met.

"I will probably never know unless my mother sells some of our cows," she said ruefully.

"Hmmm," was all Joseph could say.

"Do you not miss your family?" she asked him.

"Very much. But, even before the accident that crippled me, I knew I'd have to leave someday. I just never thought it would be in a wheelchair," he said to her.

"Montana sounds like a beautiful place," Madhu said.

"It is. I have a nephew I haven't seen since he was a few months old," Joseph said.

"Will you go back home soon?" Madhu asked.

"I don't know. Sometimes this place feels like home," he said.

"Maybe it was," Madhu offered.

"What do you mean?" Joseph asked.

"Have you ever asked Lahiri why he came looking for you? Or why he took you in to his home?" she asked.

"No. I just figured he likes to help people," Joseph replied.

"So, then he traveled halfway around the world to offer you help at a karate match, and then he also just happened to be the man you came halfway back around the world to find?" Madhu questioned.

"I don't know. I guess I just figured it was by chance," he replied.

"Nothing happens in life by chance," Madhu said.

"I guess," Joseph said.

"Maybe you were his son in a past life who died in that accident," Madhu offered.

Chapter 9

Joseph's mother stood at her kitchen counter and lifted the sliced vegetables from the cutting board onto a serving plate. She had a good many guests in her living room waiting for more appetizers. Elizabeth stood next to her, mixing homemade salad dressing, when Billy wandered in. He hoped that he could appear interested in helping without actually having to do so —cooking wasn't his thing.

"Can I help?" he asked, while straining to sound sincere but not confident that he had pulled it off.

He gave Elizabeth a kiss on the cheek for good measure. She knew exactly what he was doing, but let him off the hook just the same.

"You can help by making sure James stays out of mischief," Elizabeth said.

"How much mischief can a three-year-old get into?" he countered, feeling the need to stand up for his young son, regardless of the mischief Billy knew he was more than likely getting into.

Mrs. Connell laughed and said, "Do you remember when Joey was…"

She trailed off without finishing her question, now upset by her own memories. She stopped filling the bowl and simply stood at the counter for a moment.

Billy made his way closer to his mother and took the ladle from her hand.

"I'll do that, Mom," he said to her.

Mrs. Connell walked out of the kitchen and into the living room, where she walked under a banner that read, "Happy 25th Wedding Anniversary Bonnie & John," and feigned for some way to distract herself. Billy and Elizabeth came walking into the living room as well, each holding a bowl of food that they placed on the buffet table.

Billy quickly scanned for James, now that he had prematurely vouched for his good behavior. He found his little bundle of joy standing at a night table by the couch. The table had three pictures in frames resting on it. James picked up the one of Billy and Joseph, as Billy walked over to him and knelt beside his son. James pointed to Billy in the picture.

"That's you, Daddy," James said.

"Yes, honey, that's Daddy," Billy replied.

James pointed to Joseph.

"Who's that, Daddy?" he asked.

"That's your Uncle Joey," Billy replied.

"What's an uncle?" James asked.

Billy sighed as he replied, "That means he's my brother and your second daddy."

"Oh, where is he?" James said.

"He went away," Billy replied.

"Why?" asked the inquisitive James.

"To find himself," was all Billy could think to say.

"Did he get lost, Daddy?" James asked.

"Yes, honey, he did," Billy replied with a heavy heart.

"Why doesn't he just call?" James responded.

Billy scooped his little boy in his arms, stood up with him, and replied as much for his own comfort as his baby son's, "He will, James. He will."

Mr. Connell rang a spoon against a glass while standing under the wedding banner with his wife.

"If we could have everyone's attention, please?" he shouted.

Everyone in the house stopped their individual conversations and turned their attention toward Mr. and Mrs. Connell.

"First, to my beautiful wife, Bonnie, I want to say thank you for the priceless, twenty-five years of happiness she has given me," Mr. Connell said.

Everyone in the house clapped in agreement as Mrs. Connell gave her husband a kiss.

"And here's hoping she'll give me at least another twenty-five years," he continued as he kissed her back.

As friends continued to clap, Mr. Connell raised his glass and said, "And to our son, Joey, may we see him back home soon."

Everyone nodded in heartfelt agreement and took a sip from their drinks. Billy made his way over to his mother and father while still holding baby James in one arm and Elizabeth's hand with his free hand.

"Uh, I, uh, I mean, we, that is Elizabeth and me, we have something to add," Billy said.

He playfully pointed to himself, said, "Number one," pointed to Elizabeth and said, "Number two," pointed to James and said, "Number three," then pointed to Elizabeth's belly and said, "Number four."

For a second no one knew what Billy meant, but then all seemed to understand at the same moment and clapped loudly in approval.

Elizabeth called out to the happy room, "It's going to be a boy. Now as some of you may know, you can't actually find out the sex of the baby until the fifth month, but since this is the Connell family we're talking about here, we've already named him Thomas Joseph Connell."

Everyone was ecstatic at the news, except for Mrs. Connell, who wiped tears from her eyes as she walked out onto the wrap-around porch to be alone with her thoughts.

Madhu sat on her favorite boulder, the one that let her sit so comfortably next to Joseph in his wheel-chair. Moonlight was the only illumination, but on this night the full moon provided plenty of light.

"What made you so sure you could learn to walk when you got here?" she asked Joseph.

"I didn't know what else to do," he said. "Nothing made sense. I thought about killing myself at home, but I kept thinking about who in my family would find me and how much pain that would cause them. And I didn't have the right to do that, not after all they've done my whole life is love me. I didn't want my brother Billy to someday have to tell his son that his uncle shot himself in Grandma's house. She's al-ways loved me, even when she didn't understand me."

"And when you got here?" Madhu asked.

"Well, actually, I snuck a tiny gun to India in my wheelchair frame, and I did put it to my head and pull the trigger. But fortunately for me, Lahiri had stolen all the bullets. It wasn't because I'm a cripple. I was just so tired and wanted to rest," he said.

"It wasn't because you felt trapped?" she asked, with a slip of the tongue.

Joseph picked up on her slip, but chose not to press her on it.

"Trapped in my own life, maybe. When I was six years old, I started having nightmares. Soon they turned to more like visions that were really happening to me. At first, I just screamed in terror. I wondered if they were demons or something. When I told my mother, she eventually took me to a doctor. He put me on some drugs, but the visions only got worse...a lot worse. It was like they were trying to punish me for trying to escape them with the prescription drugs. By the time I was nine years old, I just pretended to take them. I just learned not to scream anymore. I would hold the pills under my tongue and spit them out later. Billy knew, but never told anyone," he said.

"And you never told anyone after that?" Madhu asked.

"What would have been the point? My family tried to reach me. But it was like they couldn't get in, and I couldn't get out. I never feel what I'm supposed to. I try, but I can't. And I want to so bad. But now it's too late," he lamented.

"I do not believe you cannot feel anything, Joseph" Madhu said.

"Usually the visions happened while I was sleeping, but not always. Sometimes they would take over my reality. I'd just be sitting there and suddenly I would see them. I would see someone break into our house and try to kill my family. I knew they weren't real at those times, but it still tormented me. That's why I took up karate, " he said.

"Do you think you will ever learn to walk again, really?" she asked.

"I don't know," Joseph replied. "It's not going so well and not looking like it. I don't know. I mean, I've learned some things. I've learned that we're all like leaves on that tree over there, and God is the tree, but I don't know if that has anything to do with learning to walk," he replied.

"There are more important things than walking, you know?" Madhu said.

"Like what?" Joseph asked.

"Like kissing," Madhu replied while smiling at him.

Joseph smiled brightly back at her as he leaned forward in his wheelchair. She leaned forward as well, meeting him in the middle, as they kissed gently for the first time.

W eeks later Lahiri and Joseph were out spending the afternoon by the river. Lahiri sat next to Joseph on the embankment. Across the river, a funeral was taking place. Dozens of family members and mourners gathered as four men carried the dead man and placed him on a funeral pyre—a large pile of branches that was soon to be set on fire.

"What's going on?" Joseph asked Lahiri.

"The dead man is being prepared for his death passage. Notice that he is being carried on two bamboo sticks held together by rope only," Lahiri said.

Joseph nodded his head as Lahiri continued.

"He has been washed, wrapped in a white cloth, and decorated with flowers. Relatives have placed holy water from the Ganges into his mouth for purification and to help him on his journey," Lahiri said.

Some of the deceased man's relatives said prayers while others performed ceremonial chants, while his oldest son circled his body three times, then lit his father on fire to cremate him and set his spirit free.

Lahiri leaned closer to Joseph and said, "This is the most important part, Joseph. You must remember to…I mean, the oldest son, or whoever is closest to the deceased person, must circle his body three times."

"Okay," Joseph said.

"Remember, Joseph, three times," Lahiri repeated emphatically.

"Right, three times. Got it," Joseph replied.

Joseph watched as the oldest son lit the pyre on fire in several places so that his father's body would burn as evenly as possible.

"If the deceased is believed to have obtained Moksha, the cloth wrapping the body should be yellow, instead of white," Lahiri said.

"What is Moksha?" Joseph asked.

"Moksha is the final stage of enlightenment, when enough has been learned that no future physical incarnations are necessary," Lahiri replied.

"Oh," Joseph said.

"Now, remember, Joseph, yellow, not white," Lahiri reminded him.

"Got it. Yellow, not white," Joseph said.

Later that night, Joseph sat at the desk in his room in his wheelchair, writing a letter to his mother. He was near the bottom of the page. He had been telling Mrs. Connell about how the people of India seemed to find something to celebrate nearly every single day of the year, which was probably why they had so many millions of Gods to worship. He told her about how the sweltering heat in India was matched only by the freezing cold in the winter, so high up in the Himalayan mountains. He told her how he hadn't made any progress in learning to walk through meditation, but he was starting to think that maybe he didn't really come to India to learn to walk after all.

He told his mother in his letter that maybe he really came to India to fall in love, which was beginning to happen with Madhu, he thought. He admitted that they weren't very serious yet, but that he found himself thinking about her more and more and less and less about figuring out the mind over matter trick he had come to India to learn. He also told his mother that he loved her, that he was sorry he hadn't written in so long, or hadn't told her that before. He asked her to tell his dad and Billy that he loved them too, and that he would tell them himself when he saw them again.

Off alone, on a distant mountain range Lahiri had trekked to in order to make sure he was alone, he sat meditating. Unlike his usual silent meditation, he was chanting this time. His chant started out calm and soft enough, but as he continued, his chant changed—it became louder and seemingly more insistent—more like an argument.

Lahiri argued, in his own way, that any decision such as this should be his, no one else's. He argued, in his non-verbal way, that he was the one who had orchestrated the meeting between Joseph and Madhu. He argued that what was to come was not right. He had argued, but he had lost.

Three days later, early in the morning, Lahiri stood at the table in the main room to his house. Joseph wheeled himself out from his bedroom, heartily expecting a nice breakfast. He quickly noticed that the table was empty, of everything, not just the food that wasn't there that he was expecting to see.

"Hey, what's going on? Where's breakfast?" Joseph asked.

Lahiri sighed. "Just a moment, please, Joseph," he said.

"What for?" Joseph asked again.

"Please, Joseph. Just one moment more," Lahiri replied.

Joseph waited for a moment in the silence and then there was a knock at the door. Lahiri sadly opened the door, and Joseph was shocked at who he saw standing there.

"Billy, what are you doing here?" Joseph asked.

Chapter 10

For the largest funeral procession in the memory of this small Montana town, eight pallbearers carried the oversized casket carrying John and Bonnie Connell to their final resting place in Bonnie's favorite meadow that she loved to look at from her kitchen window.

Following closely behind the pallbearers was Billy, pushing Joseph in his wheelchair, and directly behind them was Elizabeth, who carried baby Thomas Joseph as she gently held James' hand. Hundreds followed into the meadow and to the gravesite. As the pallbearers lowered the casket to the ground, Joseph huddled with Billy and his family.

The pastor led everyone in a hymn. Elizabeth cried. Billy was numb, Joseph barely under control.

As the hymn was finished, the pastor addressed the mourners.

"Our Father in Heaven, we meet this day to honor the lives of John and Bonnie Connell, and to try to offer comfort to those loved ones who are left behind, and thank Thee for all the blessings we enjoy. In the name of Jesus Christ, Amen," he said.

Larry, a close friend of the family, walked to the podium. The pastor stepped aside to let him speak.

"I have been a friend of John and Bonnie Connell since before they were married. Since we were kids. John never stormed any beaches nowhere or won any medals. I can't even remember the last time Bonnie ever traveled further than town, and even then only when she had to. They never much cared about money, no matter how much they had, but they were the richest people I have ever known, for the love they gave so freely to everyone they knew—their friends, their children, and their grandchildren," he said.

Joseph looked away and fought to not lose control. Larry's comments, while honorable to his departed friends, were cutting into him like daggers.

I know they will never be very far from us," Larry continued, "Because they live every moment with us in our hearts."

He bowed his head and stepped aside.

The pastor addressed the crowd again, "To every thing there is a season, and a time to every purpose under Heaven."

In the crowd, Billy's best friend Cody leaned over to their friend Greg.

Cody whispered to him, "Coroner pronounced them dead at the scene. Took four hours for the jaws of life to cut the car in half and get their bodies out. The drunk who hit them was singing so loud in the back of the police car, Billy went berserk, broke the window with his fist, pulled the guy out, and beat him damn near to death."

"I wondered about those bandages on his hands, until I heard what happened," Greg said.

"Guy was so drunk he didn't even remember killing Billy's parents or Billy knocking all his teeth out. Took four cops to pull Billy off a' him and Billy decked two of them before some more could wrestle him to the ground long enough for a paramedic to inject him with a sedative. D.A. wanted to press charges against Billy for assaulting the officers. Chief of Police was at Billy's baptism and his sons' baptisms. Said he'd knock the D.A.'s teeth out himself if he pressed charges against him," Cody told Greg.

Greg could only shake his head.

The pastor closed his Bible and nodded to Billy, who softly returned the nod and gently ushered his oldest son, James, forward.

The confused little boy placed a flower on top of the casket holding his dead grandparents, then stepped back to his father.

A moment later the casket was slowly lowered into ground in Mrs. Connell's favorite meadow. Joseph could barely breath.

And with that his parents were gone forever.

Back in the Connell house, mourners filled the living room. With his breathing still partly arrested, Joseph wheeled himself over to Billy and Elizabeth.

"Billy, did Mom get my letter?" Joseph asked.

Still shell-shocked, Billy replied, "What?"

Joseph grew upset with each passing moment.

"Did Mom get my letter?" he repeated emphatically.

"She didn't mention anything. Why?" Billy asked.

"Where's the mail?" Joseph implored of him.

"I put all the mail from last week in their bedroom," Billy replied.

Joseph turned his wheelchair around, using the electric switch, and headed into his parents' bedroom, oblivious to the many guests he bumped into with his chair along the way.

Billy turned in confusion to Elizabeth.

"Go after him," she said.

In his parents' bedroom, Joseph rifled through the pile of mail that Billy had left on their dresser. He found his letter…unopened. He picked it up, growing more upset with each passing moment.

Billy entered the room.

"Joey?" he softly called, unaware of the newest and most debilitating avalanche of anguish enveloping his baby brother.

Unable to speak as his jaw quivered and tears streamed into the corners of his mouth, Joseph handed his letter to Billy.

Billy opened it and scanned it top to bottom. He finally reached the part that was tearing Joseph apart. He knelt down next to Joseph's wheelchair.

"She knew, Joey. She knew. They both did, and so do I," Billy whispered.

He lowered the armrest to Joseph's wheelchair, hugged his grief-stricken brother, and wondered why life tormented him so.

Billy cradled Joseph's weary head and rocked him gently, each sob from his baby brother another knife in his already wounded heart. Billy wanted to cry, for himself, for his parents, for his brother, but that would have to wait until later.

He just held Joseph and whispered, while caressing the back of his head, "They knew, Joey. They knew."

7 Years Later

Chapter 11

As co-owner of the family bottling plant, and in his fourth year as chief financial officer, after attending college online and obtaining a finance degree, Joseph insisted on working considerably longer hours than Billy had told him would be necessary for the position. The thing was, Billy had his loving wife and two sons to go home to, and all Joseph had was the empty house he grew up in and his wheelchair.

On more than one occasion Billy also joked that going through all the trouble to dress in slacks, dress shirt, and tie wasn't necessary, after all they owned the company, but Joseph would not hear of it.

This Friday afternoon some new reports needed analysis, though the task could have waited until Monday or Tuesday. Joseph sat at his desk, on the phone, talking to an assistant in the company accounting department, when Billy wandered into his office. Joseph held up his index finger, signaling Billy that he'd be with in a moment. Billy smiled and sat down on the corner of his desk.

"Yeah, I've got the reports in front of me," Joseph said to the person on the phone he was talking with, "Now, I want you to go back and calculate the difference to projected net income under both scenarios. First under the accelerated depreciation schedule, then under a capitalized lease deal."

He waited for an answer, and then replied, "Okay, I'll be here 'til nine or so tonight. Call me if you have anything by then…. Okay, fine, call me first thing Monday."

Joseph hung up the phone and looked up at Billy, who chimed in quickly to steer the conversation away from business, "You're going to be on time for Thomas Joseph's birthday party tomorrow, right?" he asked.

"Already got his present wrapped and ready to be broken," Joseph replied.

"Does it make a lot of noise?" Billy asked, "Because Elizabeth just loves those, you know. She can't prove it, but she swears you do it on purpose."

"It does, and I do," Joseph replied, "But tell her not to worry, this one is mommy friendly."

Those reports tell you anything valuable, Mr. Slacks-And-Tie Chief Financial Officer?" Billy asked.

Joseph nodded and said, "I think the new technology's worth the investment. Net income will probably take a hit the first three years, but it looks like with fixed costs under control, variable costs go down by three or four cents per bottle, so by year four, I think, cash flow should skyrocket."

"Not bad for a guy who used to steal bottles and use them for target practice," Billy playfully jabbed.

"I schooled you, didn't I?" Joseph protested.

"So when do you fly to Utah?" Billy asked.

"Tuesday. I've got a meeting with the Lieutenant Governor and State Treasurer. If I can get them to pony up anther five million in tax breaks, we build our new plant there, if not, we'll just build it here in Montana," Joseph said.

Billy nodded, but he had now had more than his fill of shoptalk for a Friday afternoon.

"How did your date go last night?" he asked.

"I…uh…didn't go," Joseph admitted.

"Joey, why not? Jen's a great girl. She claims you sat next to her in the fifth grade and made faces at her all the time," Billy said.

"Ah, I don't know. I mean, I've gotten used to be three feet tall and all, but, I don't know," Joseph trailed off.

"Do you know she's the third girl to ask Elizabeth about you? What did you do, find their G-spot in junior high or something?" Billy asked.

Joseph laughed.

"No, I did not, that's for sure. But who has time anyway?" he said.

"Don't you want to fall in love again? Whatever happened to Madhu? Why didn't you bring her back home to Montana?" Billy asked.

Joseph was lost in thought for a moment.

"I wrote to her for years. Maybe she didn't want to leave her family? Maybe she didn't want…I don't know. I sent her money for a dowry so her mother wouldn't have to sell any of the family cows," Joseph said.

"What's a dowry?" Billy asked.

"It doesn't matter," Joseph replied.

"Right. Listen, you want to come over for dinner tonight? Elizabeth's making her world famous pot roast. The way you like it where the beef falls apart when you stick your fork in it," Billy asked.

"No, thanks, Billy. I've, uh, got to look over these reports again," Joseph replied.

"Okay. See you tomorrow then," Billy said as he stood up from the corner of Joseph's desk.

Joseph pretended to scan over the reports, but only long enough until Billy turned the corner outside his office and walked down the hallway. Then Joseph put down his pen and looked off into space, wondering about Madhu and what might have been.

The next day, Joseph was on time for his nephew's eighth birthday party, as promised. He sat on the couch in Billy's living room, next to Elizabeth's friend, Jen.

Thomas Joseph was surrounded by a dozen friends in preparation for blowing out the birthday candles on his ice cream cake.

Billy stood next to Thomas Joseph.

"Do you know what you're going to wish for?" Billy asked his son.

Thomas Joseph nodded his head that he did.

"What is it?" Billy asked him.

Older brother, James, and the mischievous one in the family, chimed in, "Don't tell. If you do it won't come true."

Billy jumped in for damage control, "James, this is a special cake, It...." he looked to Elizabeth to bail him out, but she had nothing, so he stumbled forward on his own.

"It has chocolate ice cream and the ice cream protects the wish, so it's okay," Billy said.

"That's ridiculous," James jumped in.

Billy gave James a knock it off glare, which James did.

"Go ahead, T.J.," Billy continued with his more innocent son.

"I want a Mission Soldier," Thomas Joseph replied.

Billy looked over to his wife and said, "He wants a Mission Soldier, I wonder if he'll get it?"

Elizabeth nodded yes.

"All right, T.J., if you blow out the candles real hard, I bet your wish will come true," Billy said.

Thomas Joseph blew out the candles. Billy picked his son up over his head and flew him around like an airplane.

"Time for the Mission Soldier," Billy said while flying T.J. around.

Joseph leaned towards Jen and whispered, "I think James is about ready for some Uncle interference, or I foresee a great many beautiful afternoons cleaning up more horse manure than one young boy is capable of shoveling. Maybe I'll just start slipping him a few hidden facts about his dear old dad."

"Save them," Jen replied, "You can start your uncle duties in a more important area. James has um, his first, 'official' girlfriend."

Joseph chuckled.

"He's a bit young to be embarking on that torture. What chance has a boy got? The girl has all the cards," he said.

Jen corrected him, "No, the boy has all the cards. The girl just has all the chips."

"Either way, it's a rigged game," Joseph replied.

The following day found Joseph on this beautiful Sunday afternoon driving James to his Little League baseball game. Joseph's days of driving a pickup truck were over, but his specially modified minivan worked just fine for him. Not many people believed a person could safely navigate driving a vehicle with only one usable arm. Normally a paraplegic uses his or her right hand for the gas lever on the right side of the steering wheel and his or her left hand for the brake lever on the left side. Navigating both gas and brake levers with only one hand was considered impossible, including to those people who ran the Division of Motor Vehicles Licensing Department in the county in which Joseph lived.

Their doubt was no impediment to him. As there was no law on the books prohibiting a person with only one usable limb from driving, Joseph argued that it was simply a matter of re-passing the same driver's road test he had passed as a teenager. The staff at the Motor Vehicles office saw no reason to argue with him, so they let him take the test in the minivan that had been specially modified for him.

Working the gas with his index finger, and the brake with his middle finger—an unusual talent to say the least—stunned everyone, but just as he had promised, he passed the driver's road test and was awarded a new driver's license.

James sat in the front passenger's seat in his baseball uniform, while holding his glove.

"So, James, what position do you play?" Joseph asked.

"Pitcher," James replied.

"Ah, the glory job. No one does a thing until you make the first crucial decision, what kind of pitch to throw?" Joseph responded.

"I guess," James said back.

"How's your hitting?" Joseph asked.

"Pretty good, I bat fourth," James replied.

"Fourth?! James, don't you know what that means? You're the cleanup hitter. That's more important than batting first. You must get that from me. Your dad wasn't much of an athlete. Ah…no need to tell him I said that," Joseph backpedaled.

"Now don't be fooled. He might make up some stories about playing varsity football, baseball, and wrestling all in the same year, but that doesn't prove a thing, so you don't stand for that kind of nonsense," Joseph continued.

"He told me what a great athlete you were," James said as they drove.

"He did?" Joseph asked.

"Yeah, said you were a great fighter. Still are, he said, but I don't know what that means," James replied.

"Karate," Joseph said.

James nodded his head.

"So, I hear you have your first girlfriend?" Joseph asked.

"Yeah, her name's Betsy," James replied.

"Betsy? How did you meet this Betsy?" Joseph asked.

"We played Spin the Bottle together at her house one day after school," James matter of factly replied.

"More girls than boys, I hope," Joseph said.

"Course. What do you think I am, stupid?" James responded.

"My mistake," Joseph offered.

"Anyway, she's a pretty good kisser, but I don't know. She's getting kind a' clingy. I think I like her friend Amy better," James told Joseph.

"Got any tips, kid?" Joseph mumbled.

"Her mom is driving her to the game today," James said.

"Who do you take after?" Joseph mumbled to himself again.

"Turn here, Uncle Joe, that's my team on the field over there," James said.

Hours later Joseph sat in his wheelchair back on his family's ranch, just outside the corral nearest the barn. In his hand he held a pile of carrot pieces that he was feeding to Happy, who would have come over to keep him company even without the sweet orange treats in his hand. The sun was just beginning to set over the nearest hilltop covered in the endless ponderosa pine trees.

"You, I should have taken over those hills more often when I had the chance," Joseph said to Happy.

Billy quietly walked up behind his little brother and watched him feeding his favorite horse.

"Not much of an athlete, huh?" he said to Joseph.

Joseph looked over at Billy, as his older brother made his way up next to him by the corral fence.

"I have got to teach that kid how this game is played," Joseph replied.

"And did he read something off the Internet I'm not aware of, or did you make sure he knew all the rules to spin the bottle, including the 'do-over' rule I think you made up?" Billy asked.

Joseph smiled warmly at his older brother.

"Well, I heard he's not only got his first girlfriend, but is apparently ready to move on to his second, and I didn't want him getting left behind in that arena like I did. First time I tried to kiss a girl, I got nothing but ear when she turned her head like I had the plague," Joseph said.

Billy smiled at the memory.

"Hollie. I remember that," Billy said.

"Yeah, and you were a lot of help. 'Stick your tongue down her throat. Girls love that,'" Joseph reminded Billy.

"Hey, you were thirteen and someone had to show you the ropes," Billy said in his defense.

"I was twelve, and I was lucky I remembered how to kiss Madhu," Joseph said.

Billy stopped smiling.

"You know, Joey, you never talk much about your time over there. I mean, you did spend three years of your life there," Billy said.

Joseph let out a deep sigh.

"Yeah...when I got there I thought I'd just figure out that mind over matter trick and be able to walk again no problem. But it wasn't that simple. Lahiri tried to teach me that there's more to it than that, because you have to learn something else first," Joseph finally said.

"Did you ever learn what it was?" Billy asked, intrigued.

"Yeah. But I didn't realize it until I got back home," Joseph said. "I learned that one person hurting another really is like a hand curling into a fist to smash the foot. And that all that really matters is family and other people. And that the purpose of life is to find the Light of God, but not the light from some old guy with a white beard sitting up there judging us. The light is the love we give each other on our way back home. And that God wouldn't mind if we spent a little less time telling him how great he is and a little more time loving each other, and not just the people we're supposed to love, but everyone."

Billy was stunned at the words of wisdom coming from his little brother.

"Who taught you that?" Billy asked.

"Well, Lahiri started it, but I didn't really put it all together until I got back home here, so you did... and mom and dad in their own way," Joseph said softly.

"My God, Joey, you learned more in three years over there than you did in your whole life back here," Billy said.

"Yeah, I suppose it wasn't a total waste of time," Joseph replied.

"Damn right, it wasn't. I'll tell you something else. If you can learn all that in three years over there, then you can damn well learn what you went over there for in the first place," Billy said.

"No…Billy. That was just a pipe dream that a naïve kid had a long time ago, but he's dead now," Joseph wistfully replied.

"The hell he is," Billy replied.

Billy's softness was gone, because he had made up his mind.

"You don't belong here anymore, little brother, and I won't let you stay," Bill said firmly.

Chapter 12

On the highest mountain peak that Lahiri could safely navigate Joseph's wheelchair, high enough to be among the clouds, Joseph sat meditating, breathing deeply, with a still mind and an open heart, as Lahiri guided him.

"Breathe, Joseph. Breathe deeply, and purely, and you will come to know all that you are meant to see," Lahiri said supportively.

Joseph continued breathing with sturdy determination.

"You will first begin to feel the seven chakras along your spine begin to awaken and grow in size and energy. First, they may feel no larger than a tiny pebble, but I will help you to sense them, and as they awaken and their energy grows, your insights will grow along with them. You will see that you are not a mind trapped in a body, but that the body is merely a temporary expression of your spirit," Lahiri guided him.

As Lahiri focused his mental energy on Joseph, indeed Joseph could begin to feel the spinning Wheels Of Light Lahiri described as chakras along his spine.

From the lowest spinning Wheel Of Light at the base of his spine, which was his root chakra, then up higher on his spine was the water chakra, above that the fire chakra, above that his heart chakra, still higher at the level of his Adam's apple was his throat chakra, deep within his brain at the pineal gland was the sixth chakra, known as the third eye of insight, and finally at the top of his head he could feel his crown chakra, which when sufficiently activated led to a sense of reunion with the infinite.

As Joseph sat still and "did nothing" in meditation, as ancient seers had done thousands of years before, he could see beyond the apparent limited reality that his five senses offered to him. He could feel that his body was only solid matter when viewed from without, but when viewed from within, it was a source of energy vibrations.

He could feel that his mind was not separate from his body, but that his body was merely an energetic expression of his mind, of his spirit. He could feel that the energy that made up his body—that made up the entire universe—was the energy of information traveling at different frequencies.

The longer he sat and listened from within, instead of from without, the more he could feel the energy within his body that told his heart to beat, his blood to circulate, and his eyes to blink.

He could feel that the only difference between the thoughts of his mind, between the electrical charges that traveled along his nerve cells, and between the rock mountain he sat meditating upon, was how fast or slow speed at which the energy vibrated, and so in that different speed, gave itself different expressions—be it of the slowest vibrational speed of matter, the faster vibrational speed of energy, or the finest vibrational essence of thought.

With Lahiri's assistance, Joseph could see from within that energy was merely information, the transfer of information, and that the insight of the sages could be viewed as having more access to information that permeated and constituted the known universe, not unlike a student who moves from the knowledge of simple addition and subtraction on the knowledge of advanced calculus.

The more Joseph breathed, the more he became aware, the more information he could feel from within, and finally, the more information within his being he could control from within.

Finally, he was ready to see what he was meant to know.

As he breathed the emptiness of his mind was suddenly filled with his vision of the lions that had him trapped.

As Joseph saw himself pinned under the paws of the leader of the lions, he also saw for the first time, Lahiri standing nearby in the forest. He had been present during every vision, not in physical body of course, for the visions were of energy projections only anyway. Lahiri was present via the astral energy projection of his mind. Once Lahiri had learned long ago that his mind was not confined to the apparent physical limitations of his body, his mind was free to travel anywhere he desired, and Joseph could now see that Lahiri had chosen to be with him always.

Suddenly the massive deer that had caused him to become maimed, as well as the three dead warriors that had been chasing him, all appeared next to the lions. Neither the deer nor the warriors were dead any longer. All at once, the four lions, the three warriors, and the deer all morphed back into their true forms—*spirits of White Light.*

As Joseph watched himself in the vision stand, the seven chakras, also of white light, along his spine grew in size and intensity as he remained in his wheelchair.

He watched as the spirits flew toward a misty fog and he could feel them beckoning him to follow them.

Joseph did follow them and as he crossed over to the other side of the misty fog *he could see the stone white house that he now shared with Lahiri.* Around the house were a dozen soldiers dressed in vintage military British uniforms, circa 19th century.

The soldiers carried standard single-shot rifles of the day. The white, stone house was the center of a make-shift encampment, with half a dozen simple wood and mud houses also nearby.

Directly in front of the house, Joseph saw himself as a British soldier. On his hip hung his sword—*the same sword* that he was carrying in his visions when the warrior spirits chased him in battle. He was older, in his early forties, and the highest-ranking soldier present.

Standing in front of Joseph-The-Soldier were two lower-ranking soldiers, each holding tightly the arm of an Indian man who was their prisoner. The man was intoxicated and having some difficulty standing.

Not far from Joseph-The-Soldier was Billy, also dressed in the same uniform, but of a lower rank than Joseph-The-Soldier. Bill-The-Soldier was also in his early forties.

Joseph saw himself in his vision walking closer to his former self as a British soldier. He also saw that the Indian man being held *was a younger Lahiri.*

The soldier on Lahiri's left spoke up.

"Caught him drunk and trying to incite a mutiny again, Sir," the soldier said.

"Are you most certain he was trying to incite an insurrection?" Joseph-The-Soldier asked.

"He does not deny it, Sir," the soldier replied.

Joseph-The-Soldier ruminated for a moment, but then came to a decision.

"It burdens me to say this, but…it must be done. Put him and his family to death," Joseph-The-Soldier ordered.

Bill-The-Soldier was aghast at what he had just heard.

"Joseph…I mean, Colonel Knight, may I have a word, please?" Bill-The-Soldier asked.

Joseph-The-Soldier nodded his head yes, and they both walked several feet away to speak in private.

"Please, Joseph, I beg of you, not as your junior officer, but as your friend, do not do this thing you have ordered," Bill-The-Soldier pleaded.

"It gives me no pleasure, William. I do what I must to keep civilized peace in this region. You know as well as I what happened two years ago in the Mutiny of 1857. Thousands on both sides were tortured and killed. If I do as you wish and a new mutiny spreads and thousands more die in this province that it is my sworn duty to govern, will their blood be on my hands or yours?" Joseph-The-Soldier asked.

Bill-The-Soldier was not so easily swayed from his sense of moral intervention.

"Joseph, you have ordered the murder of innocent civilians, of a mother and her two small boys, in addition to the man who is their father. We have lived more of our lives stationed here in India than in our native England. To have these people killed here now is no less heinous an act of murder than if they had been our neighbors back in Carlisle when we were just boys," Bill-The-Soldier pleaded.

"William, I mean these people no ill will. My order is not borne out of malice or disaffection for their lives, this fate they must now meet. It is unfortunate that they must perish," Joseph-The-Soldier replied.

"But they are not to 'perish' Joseph, they are to be murdered, by your order," Bill-The-Soldier argued back.

Joseph-The-Soldier was flummoxed. Had this been anyone but his best friend from boyhood, not only would the order have already been carried out, but Billy would have been brought up on charges of insubordination.

However, this was not any other soldier.

Joseph-The-Soldier walked back over to Lahiri, whose attention had by now been sobered up by the order he had heard given. The soldiers nearby, upon hearing of Joseph's order of death, had raised their rifles and pointed them at Lahiri, to ensure that no danger came to them or their commanding officer who had just made his decision.

Joseph-The-Soldier motioned for his friend Bill-The-Soldier to join him, which he did. Then Joseph-The-Soldier turned to face Lahiri.

"Sir," he said to Lahiri, "I ask you, upon your word as a gentleman, if you had not been discovered by my sentry, did you mean to bring mortal harm upon me, my men, and even upon my friend here who now pleads for the lives of your family?" Joseph-The-Soldier asked.

"Yes, I most certainly did," a defiant Lahiri icily responded.

"Why?" asked Joseph-The-Soldier.

"Because you invade our country as if it is your Divine Right to do so. You command us how to live, take what of our possessions you desire as taxes, and instruct us to be happy with what you choose to leave for us. If I invaded your country, plundered your riches, taxed your possessions, and ordered you to be happy with my presence, would you not do as I have attempted to do, even if it meant the death of me and my soldiers?" Lahiri replied.

"So I would, Sir. So I would," Joseph-The-Soldier responded respectfully.

He reached into his breast pocket and pulled out a coin, with the dated printed on it of 1859. It was the *same coin* that Joseph had found in the book he was reading in the white, stone house that belonged to Lahiri—after it had belonged to him in his past life.

He handed the coin to Lahiri.

"I respect you, Sir. For your honesty and integrity, though they may conflict with the directives of my army and even with the continuation of my life, you may use this coin to buy one last meal for your family and say a proper goodbye, compliments if her Majesty and the Crown of England," Joseph-The-Soldier said.

The two soldiers holding Lahiri escorted him away, still with rifles pointed at him by their fellow soldiers. As all the men walked further away, Joseph-The-Soldier was left alone with Bill-The-Soldier, who stared at him in disbelief.

"I do as my conscience guides me, William," Joseph-The-Soldier said.

"I fear for the fate of your soul," Bill-The-Soldier replied.

"The angels will protect me," Joseph-The-Soldier answered back.

"And if the angels attack you for what you bring to bear this day?" Bill-The-Soldier asked.

Joseph-The-Soldier moved his left hand and placed it symbolically over his sword that hung from his sash.

"Then I welcome their deeds at my place of reckoning. If there be consequences not of my desire, in this life, or in the unknown hereafter, then I accept them willingly. And if feral beasts should torment me for what I do here today, then may they at least do so where I can ride my majestic horses through the hills and enjoy the beauty of this world," Joseph-The-Soldier replied.

"I will pray for you, Joseph, as I will pray for all of us here today. You are not only my dearest friend, but you have saved my life, more than once, and for that, I will accompany you wherever your deeds and travels may take you," Bill-The-Soldier said with a heavy heart, and walked silently away.

Later that night, Joseph-The-Soldier sat at his desk in his bedroom, the same room that Lahiri had given him to use in this lifetime. He was in the midst of writing a letter on parchment paper, using a quill pen, to his superiors about the events that had taken place earlier in the day.

He paused for a moment in reflective thought, than continued writing. He expressed his sentiment that the events were unfortunate, but in his honest estimation, unavoidable.

He was about to sign his letter, when suddenly a hand reached around from behind him and dragged him to the floor.

It was an enraged Lahiri, with madness in his inflamed eyes. He beat Joseph-The-Soldier over the head several times with a wooden club, drawing significant blood, but not knocking him unconscious.

"You had my family killed! You should have had them kill me first, then I could not have escaped and now give you what you deserve!" Lahiri intoned in a low voice so nearby soldiers could not hear him.

He bashed Joseph in the head one final time, purely to inflict more pain before meting out his own form of final justice.

Lahiri began to cry uncontrollably.

"My sons were only five and two years old. They and my beautiful wife did not deserve to have their throats slashed. As you have no family for me to kill, I will send you alone to my babies and my wife, so that you may explain to them yourself why you had them murdered," Lahiri cried.

As blood flowed profusely from the head of Joseph-The-Soldier, Lahiri pulled out a twelve-inch dagger and thrust it as hard as he could into Joseph-The-Soldier's solar plexus, right at the top of the abdomen, in the exact same spot that Joseph in this lifetime was born with the pink, jagged-shaped scar at the top of his abdomen—the one Lahiri was staring at the night he approached Joseph in the locker room after his ribs had been shattered in the karate tournament.

Once the dagger was firmly in his enemy, Lahiri twisted the dagger forcefully, making sure there was no question that the wound would be fatal.

He then fled the scene of the murder.

As Joseph still sat in his wheelchair meditating, with Lahiri by his side, his vision picked up the day after his murder.

Outside the white, stone house, Bill-The-Soldier sat atop his horse. A low-ranking soldier stood in front of him, making a report to him.

"Lieutenant, Sir, we have combed this village and the surrounding areas for days. The murderer Lahiri is nowhere to be found," reported the man.

"And you are sure he is not hiding in any nearby villages?" Bill-The-Soldier asked.

"We are sure, Sir. He is somewhere," the soldier pointed off into the distant higher Himalayan mountain ranges, "deeper up there, Sir," the man responded.

"I see," Bill-The-Soldier said, sadly.

"Sir, how long do you think he can survive up there?" the soldier asked.

"A hundred years, maybe longer for all I know. However long he does survive, he will no doubt have a great many things weighing on his soul," Bill-The-Soldier replied.

"Yes, Sir," the soldier replied.

"Have the men assemble," Bill-The-Soldier ordered and gave the soldier a salute.

The soldier returned the salute, then turned and walked off in the distance to go assemble the men.

Bill-The-Soldier looked up into the nearby mountains, then up into the heavens above.

"God speed to you, Joseph. May we see each other again soon enough," Bill-The-Soldier whispered.

The vision faded as Joseph trembled in his wheelchair, reliving all the pain he had set in motion so very many years ago.

Suddenly, the disembodied spirits of Lahiri's wife and two small boys—the ones from Joseph's nightmare vision who called him Daddy, only to find their throats slashed—appeared before him.

Joseph sat in his wheelchair before them with pure sincerity. They had postponed their next bodily incarnation until his return. They had decided, rather than being reincarnated with the pain of their murder, that they would wait until he was ready to make amends for what he had done to them, so that as they progressed onto the next stage of their journey, that it would be without the burden of the pain they carried with them.

"I am sorry. I am deeply, deeply sorry for what I did to you. Please forgive me," Joseph begged from his wheelchair as they hovered in front of him.

The spirits of Lahiri's wife and two small sons did forgive Joseph, and as they did, they flew toward the heavens, to continue their journey, unburdened.

Joseph could then feel the presence of his deceased parents. He couldn't actually see their disembodied spirits, but he could feel them in his heart. He knew that they had sacrificed their physical lives for his benefit, to prevent him from unintentionally getting off course—the course of his destiny that he needed to fulfill.

Joseph felt guilty for being the cause of their deaths. His mother and father reassured him that he should not feel guilty. It was their choice, made pre-incarnation, to sacrifice their lives if necessary. The need to see through on that sacrifice did not rob them of their destiny, it helped bring it to fruition. That was why they had chosen to be his parents.

Joseph thanked his mother and father with all the love in his heart.

Suddenly, a new vision appeared before Joseph. It was of Lahiri wandering for decades up higher in the mountains, alone. After many years he gave up wandering and simply sat down to meditate. He sat for decade after decade after decade, even after he had learned what he needed to learn.

What he needed to do was wait.

Joseph could see Lahiri waiting patiently until he was reborn. Joseph could see his father and, at the time, a two-year-old Billy, standing beside Mrs. Connell in the hospital delivery room, as the newborn baby was brought back into the delivery room and handed to the beaming mother.

"Welcome to the world, baby Joseph," she said while kissing her newborn son.

The meditating Joseph could see that as the Connell family welcomed their newest edition, Lahiri rose from his meditation and walked down from the highest Himalayan mountain range, back down to the white, stone house, that had been abandoned long, long ago.

Joseph could see Lahiri sweeping the house and making repairs as the baby Joseph grew into a young boy, and he could see Lahiri planting in the garden by the house as Joseph grew into a teenager, and he could see Lahiri arrive by plane in Montana when their date with destiny was upon them.

Lahiri stood in the center of the white, stone house that had once belonged to Joseph-The-Soldier alone, then to Lahiri alone, and finally to Lahiri and Joseph together. He smiled with warmth and love as a hand gently extended toward him.

Lahiri clasped the hand of Joseph with tenderness. Forgiveness, by Lahiri for what Joseph had done to his family, and by Joseph for what Lahiri had done to him in return, was gladly given by both.

The Wheel Of Karma, that had been crushing them both beneath its suffocating weight, had finally been lifted.

In a small Montana airport, waiting at the arrival gate, a five-year-old boy jumped into his grandfather's arms.

"What are we doing here, Grandpa," the boy asked.

The grandfather was Billy, aged seventy-two years old. He was about to answer his young grandson when his elderly wife, Elizabeth, gently touched him on the arm, causing him to look up, over to the doorway that led into the airport from the plane.

Just as he did, Billy saw his baby brother, Joseph, aged seventy, slowly walking toward him.

As Joseph made his way toward the older brother he loved with all his heart, he thought about Lahiri, whom he had respectfully cremated on a funeral pyre just before leaving India for the last time. Joseph had wrapped Lahiri in the yellow cloth, as requested, for they both agreed that he had not only obtained Moksha, but most certainly earned it as well, and was now free to continue his spiritual journey without the need for further physical reincarnations.

Billy was overcome with emotion as tears welled up in his eyes and he made his way over to the baby brother he had not seen in over forty years.

As the two elderly brothers wrapped their arms around each other with as much strength as two old men could muster, a gentle smile came across Joseph's aged face. His hair had long since turned grey.

He had a face full of lines from a lifetime spent in the penetrating Indian sun, but in his eyes was the peace it took him a lifetime to earn.

Joseph rested his head on Billy's shoulder.

"Welcome home, baby brother," Billy whispered to him.

Lifting
the
Wheel
of
Karma

PAUL H. MAGID

A Reader's Guide

Reading Group Questions
&
Topics for Discussion

1. Which character was your favorite at the beginning of the novel?

2. Which character was your favorite at the end of the novel?

3. If your favorite character changed, why? Can you relate to the predicaments to your favorite character? To what extent do they remind you of yourself or someone you know?

4. Do you believe one person hurting another is like a hand curling into a fist and smashing the foot?

5. Do you believe each one of us has a Dharma in Life?

6. If you believe that we each have a Dharma—a duty, a purpose, a path—will that change how you live the rest of your Life? What do you think your Dharma could be?

7. Do you believe Joseph is right, that God wouldn't mind if we spent a little less time telling him how great he is and a little more time helping each other?

8. Do you believe forgiveness is a path to healing?

9. Could you forgive someone who had brought you so much pain?

10. Could you find the strength to ask for forgiveness from someone you may have caused such pain to?

11. Do you believe in reincarnation? If so, why? If not, why not?

12. Do you believe that some people, like Joseph's parents, come into this lifetime with the purpose of being of service to others? Even if that means sacrificing their own lives?

13. Did LIFTING THE WHEEL OF KARMA make you think about your Life? Your Path? Your Purpose? Your Duty? Your Destiny?

14. Do you believe that supernatural forces and/or spirits impact, influence, or otherwise guide the course of our lives? If you do believe this to be true, do you believe that they can be the cause of unpleasant, even painful, experiences that are nevertheless for our own benefit/good?

About The Author

Paul H. Magid started writing his debut novel, LIFTING THE WHEEL OF KARMA, twenty-five years ago while still in high school. It took him so long to complete because he tried repeatedly to abandon it, but the work refused to be forsaken. Eventually he realized that sharing this story with the world was, in fact, his Dharma.

Along the way he has worked as a Wall Street financial analyst, a waiter (not a very good one), a Hollywood Agent Trainee, a real estate developer, a summer day camp director, an award winning screenwriter, and independent filmmaker. His autobiographical film, A LIFE UNFINISHED, screened in The Hamptons International Film Festival.

Visit his website www.PaulHMagid.com

Made in the USA
Charleston, SC
24 October 2011